I0817680

TALES of the FAE

TALES of the FAE

Enchanting Stories of Fairies, Elves, and Sprites

ILLUSTRATIONS BY

Lou Benesch

CHRONICLE BOOKS
SAN FRANCISCO

Library of Congress Cataloging-in-Publication Data available.

ISBN 978-1-7972-3770-1

Manufactured in China.

Design by Kelsey Cox.
Illustrations by Lou Benesch.

10 9 8 7 6 5 4 3 2 1

Chronicle books and gifts are available at special quantity discounts to corporations, professional associations, literacy programs, and other organizations. For details and discount information, please contact our premiums department at corporategifts@chroniclebooks.com or at 1-800-759-0190.

Chronicle Books LLC
680 Second Street
San Francisco, California 94107
www.chroniclebooks.com

"Now the poor labourer was but a clumsy dancer, and he held back with a shamefaced air; but the Fairy who had been chosen to be his partner reached up and seized his hands, and lo! some strange magic seemed to enter into his veins, for in a moment he found himself waltzing and whirling, sliding and bowing, as if he had done nothing else but dance all his life."

—Elizabeth Grierson,
"The Fairies of Merlin's Crag"

CONTENTS

LOVE AND
ENCHANTMENT

THE ELFIN KNIGHT

Scotland

There is a lone moor in Scotland, which, in times past, was said to be haunted by an Elfin Knight. This Knight was only seen at rare intervals, once in every seven years or so, but the fear of him lay on all the country round, for every now and then someone would set out to cross the moor and would never be heard of again.

And although men might search every inch of the ground, no trace of him would be found, and with a thrill of horror the searching party would go home again, shaking their heads and whispering to one another that he had fallen into the hands of the dreaded Knight.

So, as a rule, the moor was deserted, for nobody dare pass that way, much less live there; and by and by it became the haunt of all sorts of wild animals, which made their lairs there, as they found that they never were disturbed by mortal huntsmen.

Now in that same region lived two young earls, Earl St. Clair and Earl Gregory, who were such friends that they rode, and hunted, and fought together, if need be.

And as they were both very fond of the chase, Earl Gregory suggested one day that they should go a-hunting on the haunted moor, in spite of the Elfin King.

"Certes, I hardly believe in him at all," cried the young man, with a laugh. "Methinks 'tis but an old wife's tale to frighten the bairns withal, lest they go straying amongst the heather and lose themselves. And 'tis pity that such fine sport should be lost because we—two bearded men—pay heed to such gossip."

But Earl St. Clair looked grave. "'Tis ill meddling with unchancy things," he answered, "and 'tis no bairn's tale that travellers have set out to cross that moor who have vanished bodily, and never mair been heard of; but it is, as thou sayest, a pity that so much good sport be lost, all because an Elfin Knight choosest to claim the land as his, and make us mortals pay toll for the privilege of planting a foot upon it.

"I have heard tell, however, that one is safe from any power that the Knight may have if one wearest the Sign of the Blessed Trinity. So let us bind That on our arm and ride forth without fear."

Sir Gregory burst into a loud laugh at these words. "Dost thou think that I am one of the bairns," he said, "first to be frightened by an idle tale, and then to think that a leaf of clover will protect me? No, no, carry that Sign if thou wilt; I will trust to my good bow and arrow."

But Earl St. Clair did not heed his companion's words, for he remembered how his mother had told him, when he was a little lad at her knee that whoso carried the Sign of the Blessed Trinity need never fear any spell that might be thrown over him by Warlock or Witch, Elf or Demon.

So he went out to the meadow and plucked a leaf of clover, which he bound on his arm with a silken scarf; then he mounted his horse and rode with Earl Gregory to the desolate and lonely moorland.

For some hours all went well; and in the heat of the chase the young men forgot their fears. Then suddenly both of them reined in their steeds and sat gazing in front of them with affrighted faces.

For a horseman had crossed their track, and they both would fain have known who he was and whence he came.

"By my troth, but he rideth in haste, whoever he may be," said Earl Gregory at last, "and tho' I always thought that no steed on earth could match mine for swiftness, I reckon that for every league that mine goeth, his would go seven. Let us follow him, and see from what part of the world he cometh."

"The Lord forbid that thou shouldst stir thy horse's feet to follow him," said Earl St. Clair devoutly. "Why, man, 'tis the Elfin Knight! Canst thou not see that he doth not ride on the solid ground, but flieth through the air, and that, although he rideth on what seemeth a mortal steed, he is really craried by mighty pinions, which cleave the air like those of a bird? Follow him forsooth! It will be an evil day for thee when thou seekest to do that."

But Earl St. Clair forgot that he carried a Talisman which his companion lacked, that enabled him to see things as they really were, while the other's eyes were holden, and he was startled and amazed when Earl Gregory said sharply, "Thy mind hath gone mad over this Elfin King. I tell thee he who passed was a goodly Knight, clad in a green vesture, and riding on a great black jennet. And because I love a gallant horseman, and would fain learn his name and degree, I will follow him till I find him, even if it be at the world's end."

And without another word he put spurs to his horse and galloped off in the direction which the mysterious stranger had taken, leaving Earl St. Clair alone upon the moorland, his fingers touching the sacred Sign and his trembling lips muttering prayers for protection.

For he knew that his friend had been bewitched, and he made up his mind, brave gentleman that he was, that he would follow him to the world's end, if need be, and try to deliver him from the spell that had been cast over him.

Meanwhile Earl Gregory rode on and on, ever following in the wake of the Knight in green, over moor, and burn, and moss, till he came to the most desolate region that he had ever been in in his life; where the wind blew cold, as if from snow-fields, and where the hoar-frost lay thick and white on the withered grass at his feet.

And there, in front of him, was a sight from which mortal man might well shrink back in awe and dread. For he saw an enormous Ring marked out on the ground, inside of which the grass, instead of being withered and frozen, was lush, and rank, and green, where hundreds of shadowy Elfin figures were dancing, clad in loose transparent robes of dull blue, which seemed to curl and twist round their wearers like snaky wreaths of smoke.

These weird Goblins were shouting and singing as they danced, and waving their arms above their heads, and throwing themselves about on the ground, for all the world as if they had gone mad; and when they saw Earl Gregory halt on his horse just outside the Ring they beckoned to him with their skinny fingers.

"Come hither, come hither," they shouted; "come tread a measure with us, and afterwards we will drink to thee out of our Monarch's loving cup."

And, strange as it may seem, the spell that had been cast over the young Earl was so powerful that, in spite of his fear, he felt that he must obey the eldrich summons, and he threw his bridle on his horse's neck and prepared to join them.

But just then an old and grizzled Goblin stepped out from among his companions and approached him.

Apparently he dare not leave the charmed Circle, for he stopped at the edge of it; then, stooping down and pretending to pick up something, he whispered in a hoarse whisper:

"I know not whom thou art, nor from whence thou comest, Sir Knight, but if thou lovest thy life, see to it that thou comest not within this Ring, nor joinest with us in our feast. Else wilt thou be for ever undone."

But Earl Gregory only laughed. "I vowed that I would follow the Green Knight," he replied, "and I will carry out my vow, even if the venture leadeth me close to the nethermost world."

And with these words he stepped over the edge of the Circle, right in amongst the ghostly dancers.

At his coming they shouted louder than ever, and danced more madly, and sang more lustily; then, all at once, a silence fell upon them, and they parted into two companies, leaving a way through their midst, up which they signed to the Earl to pass.

He walked through their ranks till he came to the middle of the Circle; and there, seated at a table of red marble, was the Knight whom he had come so far to seek, clad in his grass-green robes. And before him, on the table, stood a wondrous goblet, fashioned from an emerald, and set round the rim with blood-red rubies.

And this cup was filled with heather ale, which foamed up over the brim; and when the Knight saw Sir Gregory, he lifted it from the table, and handed it to him with a stately bow, and Sir Gregory, being very thirsty, drank.

And as he drank he noticed that the ale in the goblet never grew less, but ever foamed up to the edge; and for the first time his heart misgave him, and he wished that he had never set out on this strange adventure.

But, alas! the time for regrets had passed, for already a strange numbness was stealing over his limbs, and a chill pallor was creeping over his face, and before he could utter a single cry for help the goblet dropped from his nerveless fingers, and he fell down before the Elfin King like a dead man.

Then a great shout of triumph went up from all the company; for if there was one thing which filled their hearts with joy, it was to entice some unwary mortal into their Ring and throw their uncanny spell over him, so that he must needs spend long years in their company.

But soon their shouts of triumphs began to die away, and they muttered and whispered to each other with looks of something like fear on their faces.

For their keen ears heard a sound which filled their hearts with dread. It was the sound of human footsteps, which were so free and untrammelled that they knew at once that the stranger, whoever he was, was as yet untouched by any charm. And if this were so he might work them ill, and rescue their captive from them.

And what they dreaded was true; for it was the brave Earl St. Clair who approached, fearless and strong because of the Holy Sign he bore.

And as soon as he saw the charmed Ring and the eldrich dancers, he was about to step over its magic border, when the little grizzled Goblin who had whispered to Earl Gregory, came and whispered to him also.

"Alas! alas!" he exclaimed, with a look of sorrow on his wrinkled face, "hast thou come, as thy companion came, to pay thy toll of years to the Elfin King? Oh! if thou hast wife or child behind thee, I beseech thee, by all that thou holdest sacred, to turn back ere it be too late."

"Who art thou, and from whence hast thou come?" asked the Earl, looking kindly down at the little creature in front of him.

"I came from the country that thou hast come from," wailed the Goblin. "For I was once a mortal man, even as thou. But I set out over the enchanted moor, and the Elfin King appeared in the guise of a beauteous Knight, and he looked so brave, and noble, and generous that I followed him hither, and drank of his heather ale, and now I am doomed to bide here till seven long years be spent.

“As for thy friend, Sir Earl, he, too, hath drunk of the accursed draught, and he now lieth as dead at our lawful Monarch’s feet. He will wake up, ’tis true, but it will be in such a guise as I wear, and to the bondage with which I am bound.”

“Is there naught that I can do to rescue him?” cried Earl St. Clair eagerly, “ere he taketh on him the Elfin shape? I have no fear of the spell of his cruel captor, for I bear the Sign of One Who is stronger than he. Speak speedily, little man, for time presseth.”

“There is something that thou couldst do, Sir Earl,” whispered the Goblin, “but to essay it were a desperate attempt. For if thou failest, then could not even the Power of the Blessed Sign save thee.”

“And what is that?” asked the Earl impatiently.

“Thou must remain motionless,” answered the old man, “in the cold and frost till dawn break and the hour cometh when they sing Matins in the Holy Church. Then must thou walk slowly nine times round the edge of the enchanted Circle, and after that thou must walk boldly across it to the red marble table where sits the Elfin King. On it thou wilt see an emerald goblet studded with rubies and filled with heather ale. That must thou secure and carry away; but whilst thou art doing so let no word cross thy lips. For this enchanted ground whereon we dance may look solid to mortal eyes, but in reality it is not so. ’Tis but a quaking bog, and under it is a great lake, wherein dwelleth a fearsome Monster, and if thou so much as utter a word while thy foot resteth upon it, thou wilt fall through the bog and perish in the waters beneath.”

So saying the Grisly Goblin stepped back among his companions, leaving Earl St. Clair standing alone on the outskirts of the charmed Ring.

There he waited, shivering with cold, through the long, dark hours, till the grey dawn began to break over the hill tops, and, with its coming, the Elfin forms before him seemed to dwindle and fade away.

And at the hour when the sound of the Matin Bell came softly pealing from across the moor, he began his solemn walk. Round and round the Ring he paced, keeping steadily on his way, although loud murmurs of anger, like distant thunder, rose from the Elfin Shades, and even the very ground seemed to heave and quiver, as if it would shake this bold intruder from its surface.

But through the power of the Blessed Sign on his arm Earl St. Clair went on unhurt.

When he had finished pacing round the Ring he stepped boldly on to the enchanted ground, and walked across it; and what was his astonishment to find that all the ghostly Elves and Goblins whom he had seen, were lying frozen into tiny blocks of ice, so that he was sore put to it to walk amongst them without treading upon them.

And as he approached the marble table the very hairs rose on his head at the sight of the Elfin King sitting behind it, stiff and stark like his followers; while in front of him lay the form of Earl Gregory, who had shared the same fate.

Nothing stirred, save two coal-black ravens, who sat, one on each side of the table, as if to guard the emerald goblet, flapping their wings, and croaking hoarsely.

When Earl St. Clair lifted the precious cup, they rose in the air and circled round his head, screaming with rage, and threatening to dash it from his hands with their claws; while the frozen Elves, and even their mighty King himself stirred in their sleep, and half sat up, as if to lay hands on this presumptuous intruder. But the Power of the Holy Sign restrained them, else had Earl St. Clair been foiled in his quest.

As he retraced his steps, awesome and terrible were the sounds that he heard around him. The ravens shrieked, and the frozen Goblins screamed; and up from the hidden lake below came the sound of the deep breathing of the awful Monster who was lurking there, eager for prey.

But the brave Earl heeded none of these things, but kept steadily onwards, trusting in the Might of the Sign he bore. And it carried him safely through all the dangers; and just as the sound of the Matin Bell was dying away in the morning air he stepped on to solid ground once more, and flung the enchanted goblet from him.

And lo! every one of the frozen Elves vanished, along with their King and his marble table, and nothing was left on the rank green grass save Earl Gregory, who slowly woke from his enchanted slumber, and stretched himself, and stood up, shaking in every limb. He gazed vaguely round him, as if he scarce remembered where he was.

And when, after Earl St. Clair had run to him and had held him in his arms till his senses returned and the warm blood coursed through his veins, the two friends returned to the spot where Earl St. Clair had thrown down the wondrous goblet, they found nothing but a piece of rough grey whinstone, with a drop of dew hidden in a little crevice which was hollowed in its side.

OWAIN of DRWS COED

Wales

Until he reached the age of twenty no son could have been more devoted to his parents than Owain of Drws Coed[1]. They loved him dearly, for he was their only child, and in return for their love Owain scarcely ever left his father and mother. As soon as he had finished the work of the farm, he would come in and join the old people, talk with them, and sing in a clear, musical voice many of the songs that they rejoiced to hear. He could play on the harp, and that made his song yet more delightful for those who listened.

Sometimes the people in the village, friends of the family at Drws Coed, would come to spend the evening, and Owain sang to them as well. They begged him to sing and play on the harp, for they said, "No one sings like Owain, and his harp is very sweet." And the maidens of the village looked shyly, yet with admiration, at Owain, for he was tall and straight as an arrow, and his eyes were deep and tender in their regard. Indeed, everyone loved Owain; but Owain did not love everybody—only the dear old folk who lived in the ancient grey house of Drws Coed. So his boyhood slipped away, as the hours pass on a summer's morning, and lo! Owain was twenty.

One day the mists came rolling down the mountain-sides like great puffs of breath from a giant's mouth. Vast ragged shreds they were as they left the mountain-top, and they came down to the valley as though the giant wished to hide

---

1. Druce Koid, door of wood

the whole world from his view. Owain led his sheep lower down the slope, because the mist had laid thousands of sparkling drops upon the grass, and moss-covered rocks, and also on the backs of the sheep; and there was no blue sky to be seen anywhere. He wished to find a sheltered spot in the well-known valley where the flock could be safely shut in a pen. As he drove them before him he reached Cwm Marchnad,[2] where the reeds grow tall and rich, and the ground is always marshy. Owain little thought what was awaiting him in this place; but he went on, driving his sheep before him, and thinking of the old folk at home.

Then, all at once, his eye beheld under the shelter of a large, grassy mound a figure which made his heart throb and leap within him. It was a young and exceedingly beautiful woman. Never had Owain dreamed that such beauty could be upon our earth; for this lass as much surpassed the gentle maids of the village as the delicate, winning wild-rose surpassed the wool flowers his mother worked into her patterns. He could only stand and stare at her with all his might, as though he wished his eyes could drink in all her beauty.

Her hair was very long, and lay about her in curling masses of fine golden threads. So very golden was it that it seemed to have caught some of the rays of the hidden sun. Her eyes were as blue and sparkling as the summer skies, and her forehead was as white as the foam that dwells on the leaping wave, or as the snow new fallen from heaven. Her face was rounded with the fresh beauty of youth, and her cheek blushed like the red roses of summer, and as Owain looked at her lips, which were small and perfectly shaped, and rich in colour, he thought they were so pretty that even an angel would desire to kiss them. Yet Owain had never before had the thought of love in his heart, and he loved best of all to sing and play the harp to the old people at Drws Coed. But now love had surged through his veins as the rich light of the early summer floods the fields of young corn, and ripens them to harvest. He was heartstricken; yea, he who was so timid and shy drew near to the wondrous girl, as pieces of paper fly towards amber. In faltering words, and speaking rather with his eyes than with his voice, he asked her whether he might stay and converse with her. She smiled courteously upon him, and, reaching forth

2. Koom Marchnad, valley of the market.

a hand pure white as the drooping snowdrop, took his rough, red hand and said, "Idol of my hopes, thou hast come at last!"

Then Owain's tongue lost its fear, and the words flowed smoothly as the brook which has reached the valley. He spoke of love and the springtide, of his father and mother at home, and the old grey farm of Drws Coed; and the maiden sat and listened with her gentle hands folded in her lap, and her eyes, tender and sweet, watching his lips as they formed the words and disclosed his white teeth. Ever and anon she smiled at his beauty, as he marvelled at hers; and so the hours slipped swiftly away.

Not far away along the valley was the Llyn y Gadair,[3] a lake that lay all shut in by the protecting mountains. Here there was perfect peace, silence like the silence of Heaven, and the beauty of nature at her sweetest and best. Around the silvery margin of the lake stood young groves of birch-trees, whose white barks were flaky with the swelling wood, and beyond these groves lay fields which were clothed in the spring with the purity of the daisy and the gleam of the golden buttercup. Hither Owain and Bela would wander, hand in hand, speechless, yet by their glances telling more than words could express, and forgetful of the worlds above and below.

At last, Love so much overcame Owain that he was restless day and night when Bela was absent from him. Sometimes, ere yet it was dawn, he would arise and sing:

"O sweeter to me is the face of my Fair,
More beautiful far than the rose;
More golden than sunshine the strands of her hair,
When day draweth near to a close.

Like fire in the heart is my Love, when 'tis day,
And Love filleth my soul in the night.
Then hearing these words, Love, O do not delay,
But come with thy glances so bright."

---

3. Llin e gadair, lake of the chair.

And Owain's father and mother and his many friends thought the black-haired boy was bewitched, for thus he sang in the night, while by day he would wander away for long spells, and no one could tell whither he had gone, nor what had become of him.

But at length the secret lay open, and all knew of Owain's love. Yet before Owain told his story he and Bela had passed through a long and loving courtship by the Llyn y Gadair. For thither would Owain turn his steps, and there was Bela always awaiting him. For this reason the place of their tryst has been known as the Maiden's Bower, and in this sacred haunt the young lovers spent the golden hours of youth, and determined, as time went on, to marry.

But if they were to marry it was necessary for Bela to obtain her father's consent, and who could tell how he would view her love for Owain? Yet she told him; and the word came to Owain to await her father in the woods. Accordingly, on the night when the full moon floated in the sky, Owain went out and waited to hear his fate, and stood long and anxiously among the silver birches, while nature slept, and the moonlight danced on the ripples of Llyn y Gadair.

For a long time there was no sign of living person other than himself; but as the moon passed over and beyond the mountain-side, there came towards him two forms. By the soft misty hair Owain recognised the beautiful Bela. Her head bent low as she drew near to her lover. The other form was that of an old man, with a kindly peaceful face and silver-streaming hair. He came gently up to Owain, and taking the lad's hand placed within it the white hand of Bela. Then he said: "Thou shalt have my daughter, Owain, but on one condition only. Never shalt thou allow cold iron to touch her flesh. If thou dost, then she shall no longer be thine, but shall return at once to her own people."

Then Owain was blithe at heart, and his voice was as the flow of the nightingale's song when all the woods are hushed to hear it sing its lay of love. Gladly he consented to the condition. There was no talk about any dowry, for love was the only acceptable one. Then the silver-haired old father led away the shy and lovely Bela. Yet before they departed, Owain and she had fixed the day for their marriage.

On the appointed day they were married, and all those present at the ceremony declared that they had never seen at the altar a more handsome or fairer couple.

People tell how a large sum of money came with Bela as her dowry; for the people of Tylwyth Têg are as wealthy as those who dwell among the hills of gold, and on the wedding night the charming virgin went to Drws Coed, rich in the golden offerings of her kinsfolk. And very soon after that the young master shepherd of Cwm Marchnad was a rich and responsible man.

After the fashion of nature, in due time children were born to Owain and Bela, and they and their family lived happily together. Everything passed in sweet contentment for many a year. Yes, indeed, wealth poured in continually, for Fortune is a wondrous dame. She is the eldest daughter of Providence, and to her, as to her mother, are entrusted marvellous treasures to impart them as she is disposed. The old proverb says that water runs down to the valley, and so it was with this couple. They became wealthy beyond the average lot of man.

But the fair rose hath her sting; night will ever follow day. One cannot have the sweet without the bitter, and even so it came to pass for Owain and Bela.

One day the husband and wife chanced to ride out and visit the cherished margin of Llyn y Gadair. As they rode, Bela went too near the water, and, its foot slipping, her horse sank into the water up to its girth. Owain hastened to save his dear wife, and, when the horse was safely on shore again, he helped Bela to get off her wet steed and mount his own. Alack the day! in his hurry to place her little foot in the stirrup, the iron slipped and just touched her knee. They looked at one another with faces pale as the mistletoe-berry, and hastened to gallop home.

Ere they had reached half-way, there stole down the hill-side the strains of sweetest music. Rippling and entrancingly it came, wreathing and folding in its gentle murmurs and tender cadences everything around the mountain foot. And, as the harmonies sank into Owain's soul, he saw that they were surrounded with a myriad of the "small people," while others came rushing down the hill-side. They looked at him, and the tears stole down from their eyes. They took Bela gently in their arms and the air was full of sad farewells to Owain. Then as the mist comes suddenly and obscures the view, so Owain stood looking at the empty saddle of his dear wife's horse. Bela, his beautiful, loving Bela, had passed away before his sight, and he knew not where to seek her.

Some people in the district say that she was taken to the Maiden's Bower, and thence to the land of Hud, that she left her dear little ones to the care of her beloved, and that she came no more to their presence. But there are others who speak with more confidence and narrate a happier story, for they tell how every now and again Owain and his little ones would catch a glimpse of the lovely Bela. And it happened in this wise. Since the laws of her country forbade her to tread the earth with any human being, as she had been touched with iron, she and her mother thought long and earnestly, and at last they contrived a way in which she could see and converse with her husband and children once again. They obtained a large turf—great enough to float and at the same time support Bela. This they were wont to place on the surface of the lake not far from the silver strand, and here she would sit almost within reach of her dear ones, and for long, sweet hours hold loving talk with them. Thus they all lived together till time loosened Owain's soul, and it passed away on the breeze of the morning.

TAMLANE

England

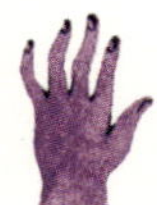

Young Tamlane was son of Earl Murray, and Burd Janet was daughter of Dunbar, Earl of March. And when they were young they loved one another and plighted their troth. But when the time came near for their marrying, Tamlane disappeared, and none knew what had become of him.

Many, many days after he had disappeared, Burd Janet was wandering in Carterhaugh Wood, though she had been warned not to go there. And as she wandered she plucked the flowers from the bushes. She came at last to a bush of broom and began plucking it. She had not taken more than three flowerets when by her side up started young Tamlane.

"Where come ye from, Tamlane, Tamlane?" Burd Janet said; "and why have you been away so long?"

"From Elfland I come," said young Tamlane. "The Queen of Elfland has made me her knight."

"But how did you get there, Tamlane?" said Burd Janet.

"I was a-hunting one day, and as I rode widershins round yon hill, a deep drowsiness fell upon me, and when I awoke, behold! I was in Elfland. Fair is that land and gay, and fain would I stop but for thee and one other thing. Every seven years the Elves pay their tithe to the Nether world, and for all the Queen makes much of me, I fear it is myself that will be the tithe."

"Oh can you not be saved? Tell me if aught I can do will save you, Tamlane?"

"One only thing is there for my safety. To-morrow night is Hallowe'en, and the fairy court will then ride through England and Scotland, and if you would borrow me from Elfland you must take your stand by Miles Cross between twelve and one o' the night, and with holy water in your hand you must cast a compass all around you."

"But how shall I know you, Tamlane?" quoth Burd Janet, "amid so many knights I've ne'er seen before?"

"The first court of Elves that come by let pass, let pass. The next court you shall pay reverence to, but do naught nor say aught. But the third court that comes by is the chief court of them, and at the head rides the Queen of all Elfland. And by her side I shall ride upon a milk-white steed with a star in my crown; they give me this honour as being a christened knight. Watch my hands, Janet, the right one will be gloved but the left one will be bare, and by that token you will know me."

"But how to save you, Tamlane?" quoth Burd Janet.

"You must spring upon me suddenly, and I will fall to the ground. Then seize me quick, and whatever change befall me, for they will exercise all their magic on me, cling hold to me till they turn me into red-hot iron. Then cast me into this pool and I will be turned back into a mother-naked man. Cast then your green mantle over me, and I shall be yours, and be of the world again."

So Burd Janet promised to do all for Tamlane, and next night at midnight she took her stand by Miles Cross and cast a compass round her with holy water.

Soon there came riding by the Elfin court; first over the mound went a troop on black steeds, and then another troop on brown. But in the third court, all on milk-white steeds, she saw the Queen of Elfland and by her side a knight with a star in his crown, with right hand gloved and the left bare. Then she knew this was her own Tamlane, and springing forward she seized the bridle of the milk-white steed and pulled its rider down. And as soon as he had touched the ground she let go the bridle and seized him in her arms.

"He's won, he's won amongst us all," shrieked out the eldritch crew, and all came around her and tried their spells on young Tamlane.

First they turned him in Janet's arms like frozen ice, then into a huge flame of roaring fire. Then, again, the fire vanished and an adder was skipping through her arms, but still she held on; and then they turned him into a snake that reared up as if to bite her, and yet she held on. Then suddenly a dove was struggling in her arms, and almost flew away. Then they turned him into a swan, but all was in vain, till at last he was changed into a red-hot glaive, and this she cast into a well of water and then he turned back into a mother-naked man. She quickly cast her green mantle over him, and young Tamlane was Burd Janet's for ever.

Then sang the Queen of Elfland as the court turned away and began to resume its march.

"She that has borrowed young Tamlane
Has gotten a stately groom,
She's taken away my bonniest knight
Left nothing in his room.

"But had I known, Tamlane, Tamlane,
A lady would borrow thee,
I'd hae ta'en out thy two grey eyne,
Put in two eyne of tree.

"Had I but known, Tamlane, Tamlane,
Before we came from home,
I'd hae ta'en out thy heart o' flesh,
Put in a heart of stone.

"Had I but had the wit yestreen
That I have got to-day,
I'd paid the Fiend seven times his teind
Ere you'd been won away."

And then the Elfin court rode away, and Burd Janet and young Tamlane went their way homewards and were soon after married after young Tamlane had again been sained by the holy water and made Christian once more.

CHILDE ROWLAND

England

Childe Rowland and his brothers twain
Were playing at the ball.
Their sister, Burd Helen, she played
In the midst among them all.

For Burd Helen loved her brothers and they loved her exceedingly. At play she was ever their companion and they cared for her as brothers should. And one day when they were at ball close to the churchyard—

Childe Rowland kicked it with his foot
And caught it on his knee.
At last as he plunged among them all,
O'er the church he made it flee.

Now Childe Rowland was Burd Helen's youngest, dearest brother, and there was ever a loving rivalry between them as to which should win. So with a laugh—

Burd Helen round about the aisle
To seek the ball is gone.

Now the ball had trundled to the right of the church; so, as Burd Helen ran the nearest way to get it, she ran contrary to the sun's course, and the light, shining full on her face, sent her shadow behind her. Thus that happened which will happen at times when folk forget and run widershins, that is against the light, so that their shadows are out of sight and cannot be taken care of properly.

Now what happened you will learn by and by; meanwhile, Burd Helen's three brothers waited for her return.

> But long they waited, and longer still,
> And she came not back again.

Then they grew alarmed, and—

> They sought her east, they sought her west,
> They sought her up and down.
> And woe were the hearts of her brethren,
> Since she was not to be found.

Not to be found anywhere—she had disappeared like dew on a May morning.

So at last her eldest brother went to Great Merlin the Magician, who could tell and foretell, see and foresee all things under the sun and beyond it, and asked him where Burd Helen could have gone.

"Fair Burd Helen," said the Magician, "must have been carried off with her shadow by the fairies when she was running round the church widershins; for fairies have power when folk go against the light. She will now be in the Dark Tower of the King of Elfland, and none but the boldest knight in Christendom will be able to bring her back."

"If it be possible to bring her back," said the eldest brother, "I will do it, or perish in the attempt."

"Possible it is," quoth Merlin the Magician gravely. "But woe be to the man or mother's son who attempts the task if he be not well taught beforehand what he is to do."

Now the eldest brother of fair Burd Helen was brave indeed, danger did not dismay him, so he begged the Magician to tell him exactly what he should do, and what he should not do, as he was determined to go and seek his sister. And the Great Magician told him, and schooled him, and after he had learnt his lesson right well he girt on his sword, said good-bye to his brothers and his mother, and set out for the Dark Tower of Elfland to bring Burd Helen back.

But long they waited, and longer still,
With doubt and muckle pain.
But woe were the hearts of his brethren,
For he came not back again.

So after a time Burd Helen's second brother went to Merlin the Magician and said:

"School me also, for I go to find my brother and sister in the Dark Tower of the King of Elfland and bring them back." For he also was brave indeed, danger did not dismay him.

Then when he had been well schooled and had learnt his lesson, he said good-bye to Childe Rowland, his brother, and to his mother the good Queen, girt on his sword, and set out for the Dark Tower of Elfland to bring back Burd Helen and her brother.

But long they waited, and longer still,
With muckle doubt and pain.
And woe were his mother's and brother's hearts,
For he came not back again.

Now when they had waited and waited a long, long time, and none had come back from the Dark Tower of Elfland, Childe Rowland, the youngest, the best beloved of Burd Helen's brothers, besought his mother to let him also go on the quest; for he was the bravest of them all, and neither death nor danger could dismay him. But at first his mother the Queen said:

"Not so! You are the last of my children; if you are lost, all is lost indeed!"

But he begged so hard that at length the good Queen his mother bade him God-speed, and girt about his waist his father's sword, the brand that never struck in vain, and as she girt it on she chanted the spell that gives victory.

So Childe Rowland bade her good-bye and went to the cave of the Great Magician Merlin.

"Yet once more, Master," said the youth, "and but once more, tell how man or mother's son may find fair Burd Helen and her brothers twain in the Dark Tower of Elfland."

"My son," replied the wizard Merlin, "there be things twain; simple they seem to say, but hard are they to perform. One thing is to do, and one thing is not to do. Now the first thing you have to do is this: After you have once entered the Land of Faery, *whoever speaks to you*, you must out with your father's brand and cut off their head. In this you must not fail. And the second thing you have not to do is this: After you have entered the Land of Faery, bite no bit, sup no drop; for if in Elfland you sup one drop or bite one bit, never again will you see Middle Earth."

Then Childe Rowland said these two lessons over and over until he knew them by heart; so, well schooled, he thanked the Great Master and went on his way to seek the Dark Tower of Elfland.

And he journeyed far, and he journeyed fast, until at last on a wide moorland he came upon a horse-herd feeding his horses; and the horses were wild, and their eyes were like coals of fire.

Then he knew they must be the horses of the King of Elfland, and that at last he must be in the Land of Faery.

So Childe Rowland said to the horse-herd, "Canst tell me where lies the Dark Tower of the Elfland King?"

And the horse-herd answered, "Nay, that is beyond my ken; but go a little farther and thou wilt come to a cow-herd who mayhap can tell thee."

Then at once Childe Rowland drew his father's sword that never struck in vain, and smote off the horse-herd's head, so that it rolled on the wide moorland and frightened the King of Elfland's horses. And he journeyed further till he came to a wide pasture where a cow-herd was herding cows. And the cows looked at him with fiery eyes, so he knew that they must be the King of Elfland's cows, and that he was still in the Land of Faery. Then he said to the cow-herd:

"Canst tell me where lies the Dark Tower of the Elfland King?"

And the cow-herd answered, "Nay, that is beyond my ken; but go a little farther and thou wilt come to a hen-wife who, mayhap, can tell thee."

So at once Childe Rowland, remembering his lesson, out with his father's good sword that never struck in vain, and off went the cow-herd's head spinning amongst the grasses and frightening the King of Elfland's cows.

Then he journeyed further, till he came to an orchard where an old woman in a grey cloak was feeding fowls. And the fowls' little eyes were like little coals of fire, so he knew that they were the King of Elfland's fowls, and that he was still in the Land of Faery.

And he said to the hen-wife, "Canst tell me where lies the Dark Tower of the King of Elfland?"

Now the hen-wife looked at him and smiled. "Surely I can tell you," said she; "go on a little farther. There you will find a low green hill; green and low against the sky. And the hill will have three terrace-rings upon it from bottom to top. Go round the first terrace saying:

'Open from within;
Let me in! Let me in!'

Then go round the second terrace and say:

'Open wide, open wide.
Let me inside.'

Then go round the third terrace and say:

'Open fast, open fast,
Let me in at last.'

Then a door will open and let you in to the Dark Tower of the King of Elfland. Only remember to go round widershins. If you go round with the sun the door will not open. So good luck to you!"

Now the hen-wife spoke so fair, and smiled so frank, that Childe Rowland forgot for a moment what he had to do. Therefore he thanked the old woman for her courtesy and was just going on, when, all of a sudden, he remembered his lesson. And he out with his father's sword that never yet struck in vain, and smote off the hen-wife's head, so that it rolled among the corn and frightened the fiery-eyed fowls of the King of Elfland.

After that he went on and on, till, against the blue sky, he saw a round green hill set with three terraces from top to bottom.

Then he did as the hen-wife had told him, not forgetting to go round widershins, so that the sun was always on his face.

Now when he had gone round the third terrace saying:

"Open fast, open fast,
Let me in at last,"

what should happen but that he should see a door in the hill-side. And it opened and let him in. Then it closed behind him with a click, and Childe Rowland was left in the dark; for he had gotten at last to the Dark Tower of the King of Elfland.

It was very dark at first, perhaps because the sun had part blinded his eyes; for after a while it became twilight, though where the light came from none could tell, unless through the walls and the roof; for there were neither windows nor candles. But in the gloaming light he could see a long passage of rough arches made of rock that was transparent and all encrusted with sheep-silver, rock-spar, and many bright stones. And the air was warm as it ever is in Elfland. So he went on and on in the twilight that came from nowhere, till he found himself before two wide doors all barred with iron. But they flew open at his touch and he saw a wonderful, large, and spacious hall that seemed to him to be as long and as broad as the green hill itself. The roof was supported by pillars wide and lofty beyond the pillars of a cathedral; and they were of gold and silver, fretted into foliage, and between and around them were woven wreaths of flowers. And the flowers were of diamonds, and rubies, and topaz, and the leaves of emerald. And the arches met in the middle of the roof where hung, by a golden chain, an immense lamp made of a hollowed pearl, white and translucent. And in the middle of this lamp was a mighty carbuncle, blood-red, that kept spinning round and round, shedding its light to the very ends of the huge hall, which thus seemed to be filled with the shining of the setting sun.

Now at one end of the hall was a marvellous, wondrous, glorious couch of velvet, and silk, and gold; and on it sate fair Burd Helen combing her beautiful golden hair with a golden comb. But her face was all set and wan, as if it were made of stone. And when she saw Childe Rowland she never moved, and her voice came like the voice of the dead as she said:

"God pity you, poor luckless fool!
What have you here to do?"

Now at first Childe Rowland felt he must clasp this semblance of his dear sister in his arms; but he remembered the lesson which the Great Magician Merlin had taught him, and drawing his father's brand which had never yet been drawn in vain, and turning his eyes from the horrid sight, he struck with all his force at the enchanted form of fair Burd Helen.

And lo! when he turned to look in fear and trembling, there she was her own self, her joy fighting with her fears. And she clasped him in her arms and cried:

"Oh, hear you this, my youngest brother,
Why didn't you bide at home?
Had you a hundred thousand lives,
Ye couldn't spare ne'er a one!

"But sit you down, my dearest dear,
Oh! woe that ye were born,

For, come the King of Elfland in
Your fortune is forlorn."

So with tears and smiles she seated him beside her on the wondrous couch, and they told each other what they each had suffered and done. He told her how he had come to Elfland, and she told him how she had been carried off, shadow and all, because she ran round a church widershins, and how her brothers had been enchanted, and lay intombed as if dead, as she had been, because they had not had the courage to obey the Great Magician's lesson to the letter, and cut off her head.

Now after a time Childe Rowland, who had travelled far and travelled fast, became very hungry, and forgetting all about the second lesson of the Magician Merlin, asked his sister for some food. And she, being still under the spell of Elfland could not warn him of his danger; she could only look at him sadly as she rose up and brought him a golden basin full of bread and milk.

Now in those days it was manners before taking food from any one to say thank you with your eyes, and so just as Childe Rowland was about to put the golden bowl to his lips, he raised his eyes to his sister's.

And in an instant he remembered what the Great Magician had said: "Bite no bit, sup no drop, for if in Elfland you sup one drop or bite one bit, never again will you see Middle Earth."

So he dashed the bowl to the ground, and standing square and fair, lithe, and young, and strong, he cried like a challenge:

"Not a sup will I swallow, not a bit will I bite till fair Burd Helen is set free."

Then immediately there was a loud noise like thunder, and a voice was heard saying:

"Fee, fo, fi, fum,
I smell the blood of a Christian Man.
Be he alive or dead, my brand
Shall dash his brains from his brain-pan."

Then the folding-doors of the vast hall burst open and the King of Elfland entered like a storm of wind. What he was really like Childe Rowland had not time to see, for with a bold cry:

"Strike, Bogle! thy hardest if thou dar'st!" he rushed to meet the foe, his good sword, that never yet did fail, in his hand.

And Childe Rowland and the King of Elfland fought, and fought, and fought, while Burd Helen, with her hands clasped, watched them in fear and hope.

So they fought, and fought, and fought, until at last Childe Rowland beat the King of Elfland to his knees. Whereupon he cried, "I yield me. Thou hast beaten me in fair fight."

Then Childe Rowland said, "I grant thee mercy if thou wilt release my sister and my brothers from all spells and enchantments, and let us go back to Middle Earth."

So that was agreed; and the Elfin King went to a golden chest whence he took a phial that was filled with a blood-red liquor. And with this liquor he anointed the ears and the eyelids, the nostrils, the lips, and the finger-tips of the bodies of Burd Helen's two brothers that lay as dead in two golden coffers.

And immediately they sprang to life and declared that their souls only had been away, but had now returned.

After this the Elfin King said a charm which took away the very last bit of enchantment, and adown the huge hall that showed as if it were lit by the setting sun, and through the long passage of rough arches made of rock that was transparent and all encrusted with sheep-silver, rock-spar, and many bright stones, where twilight reigned, the three brothers and their sister passed. Then the door opened in the green hill, it clicked behind them, and they left the Dark Tower of the King of Elfland never to return.

For, no sooner were they in the light of day, than they found themselves at home.

But fair Burd Helen took care never to go widershins round a church again.

TROUBLESOME
NEIGHBORS

THE FAIRIES of MERLIN'S CRAG

Scotland

About two hundred years ago there was a poor man working as a labourer on a farm in Lanarkshire. He was what is known as an "orra man"; that is, he had no special work mapped out for him to do, but he was expected to undertake odd jobs of any kind that happened to turn up.

One day his master sent him out to cast peats on a piece of moorland that lay on a certain part of the farm. Now this strip of moorland ran up at one end to a curiously shaped crag, known as Merlin's Crag, because, so the country folk said, that famous Enchanter had once taken up his abode there.

The man obeyed, and, being a willing fellow, when he arrived at the moor he set to work with all his might and main. He had lifted quite a quantity of peat from near the Crag, when he was startled by the appearance of the very smallest woman that he had ever seen in his life. She was only about two feet high, and she was dressed in a green gown and red stockings, and her long yellow hair was not bound by any ribbon, but hung loosely round her shoulders.

She was such a dainty little creature that the astonished countryman stopped working, stuck his spade into the ground, and gazed at her in wonder.

His wonder increased when she held up one of her tiny fingers and addressed him in these words: "What wouldst thou think if I were to send my husband to uncover thy house? You mortals think that you can do aught that pleaseth you."

Then, stamping her tiny foot, she added in a voice of command, "Put back that turf instantly, or thou shalt rue this day."

Now the poor man had often heard of the Fairy Folk and of the harm that they could work to unthinking mortals who offended them, so in fear and trembling he set to work to undo all his labour, and to place every divot in the exact spot from which he had taken it.

When he was finished he looked round for his strange visitor, but she had vanished completely; he could not tell how, nor where. Putting up his spade, he wended his way homewards, and going straight to his master, he told him the whole story, and suggested that in future the peats should be taken from the other end of the moor.

But the master only laughed. He was a strong, hearty man, and had no belief in Ghosts, or Elves, or Fairies, or any other creature that he could not see; but although he laughed, he was vexed that his servant should believe in such things, so to cure him, as he thought, of his superstition, he ordered him to take a horse and cart and go back at once, and lift all the peats and bring them to dry in the farm steading.

The poor man obeyed with much reluctance; and was greatly relieved, as weeks went on, to find that, in spite of his having done so, no harm befell him.

In fact, he began to think that his master was right, and that the whole thing must have been a dream.

So matters went smoothly on. Winter passed, and spring, and summer, until autumn came round once more, and the very day arrived on which the peats had been lifted the year before.

That day, as the sun went down, the orra man left the farm to go home to his cottage, and as his master was pleased with him because he had been working very hard lately, he had given him a little can of milk as a present to carry home to his wife.

So he was feeling very happy, and as he walked along he was humming a tune to himself. His road took him by the foot of Merlin's Crag, and as he approached it he was astonished to find himself growing strangely tired. His eyelids dropped over his eyes as if he were going to sleep, and his feet grew as heavy as lead.

"I will sit down and take a rest for a few minutes," he said to himself; "the road home never seemed so long as it does to-day."

So he sat down on a tuft of grass right under the shadow of the Crag, and before he knew where he was he had fallen into a deep and heavy slumber.

When he awoke it was near midnight, and the moon had risen on the Crag. And he rubbed his eyes, when by its soft light he became aware of a large band of Fairies who were dancing round and round him, singing and laughing, pointing their tiny fingers at him, and shaking their wee fists in his face.

The bewildered man rose and tried to walk away from them, but turn in whichever direction he would the Fairies accompanied him, encircling him in a magic ring, out of which he could in no wise go.

At last they stopped, and, with shrieks of elfin laughter, led the prettiest and daintiest of their companions up to him, and cried, "Tread a measure, tread a measure, Oh, Man! Then wilt thou not be so eager to escape from our company."

Now the poor labourer was but a clumsy dancer, and he held back with a shamefaced air; but the Fairy who had been chosen to be his partner reached up and seized his hands, and lo! some strange magic seemed to enter into his veins, for in a moment he found himself waltzing and whirling, sliding and bowing, as if he had done nothing else but dance all his life.

And, strangest thing of all! he forgot about his home and his children; and he felt so happy that he had no longer the slightest desire to leave the Fairies' company.

All night long the merriment went on. The Little Folk danced and danced as if they were mad, and the farm man danced with them, until at last a shrill sound came over the moor. It was the cock from the farmyard crowing its loudest to welcome the dawn.

In an instant the revelry ceased, and the Fairies, with cries of alarm, crowded together and rushed towards the Crag, dragging the countryman along in their midst. As they reached the rock, a mysterious door, which he never remembered having seen before, opened in it of its own accord, and shut again with a crash as soon as the Fairy Host had all trooped through.

The door led into a large, dimly lighted hall full of tiny couches, and here the Little Folk sank to rest, tired out with their exertions, while the good man sat down on a piece of rock in the corner, wondering what would happen next.

But there seemed to be some kind of spell thrown over his senses, for even when the Fairies awoke and began to go about their household occupations, and to carry out certain curious practices which he had never seen before, and which, as you will hear, he was forbidden to speak of afterwards, he was content to sit and watch them, without in any way attempting to escape.

As it drew toward evening someone touched his elbow, and he turned round with a start to see the little woman with the green dress and scarlet stockings, who had remonstrated with him for lifting the turf the year before, standing by his side.

"The divots which thou took'st from the roof of my house have grown once more," she said, "and once more it is covered with grass; so thou canst go home again, for justice is satisfied—thy punishment hath lasted long enough. But first must thou take thy solemn oath never to tell to mortal ears what thou hast seen whilst thou hast dwelt among us."

The countryman promised gladly, and took the oath with all due solemnity. Then the door was opened, and he was at liberty to depart.

His can of milk was standing on the green, just where he had laid it down when he went to sleep; and it seemed to him as if it were only yesternight that the farmer had given it to him.

But when he reached his home he was speedily undeceived. For his wife looked at him as if he were a ghost, and the children whom he had left wee, toddling things were now well-grown boys and girls, who stared at him as if he had been an utter stranger.

"Where hast thou been these long, long years?" cried his wife when she had gathered her wits and seen that it was really he, and not a spirit. "And how couldst thou find it in thy heart to leave the bairns and me alone?"

And then he knew that the one day he had passed in Fairy-land had lasted seven whole years, and he realised how heavy the punishment had been which the Wee Folk had laid upon him.

FAIRY COWS

Ireland

In the parish of Drummor lived a farmer, whose name was Tom Connors. He had a nice bit of land and four cows. He was a fine, strong, honest man, and had a wife and five children.

Connors had one cow which was better than the other three, and she went by the name of Cooby. She got that name because her two horns turned in toward her eyes. They used to feed her often at the house, and she was very gentle, and had a heifer calf every year for five or six years.

On one corner of Connors's farm there was a fairy fort, and the cow Cooby used to go into the fort, but Connors always drove her out, and told his wife and boys to keep her away from the fort, "for," said he, "it isn't much luck there is for any cow or calf that is fond of going into these fairy forts."

Soon they noticed that Cooby's milk was failing her and that she was beginning to pine away, and though she had the same food at home as before, nothing would do her but to go to the fort.

One morning when Connors went to drive his cows home to be milked he found Cooby in the field and her forelegs broken. He ran home that minute for a knife, killed and skinned the cow, made four parts of the carcase, put the pieces in a hamper, and carried the hamper home on his back.

What of the meat himself and family didn't eat fresh he salted, and now and then of a Sunday evening or a holiday they had a meal of it with cabbage, and it lasted a long time.

One morning after Tom was gone to the bog to cut turf the wife went out to milk, and what should she see but a cow walking into the fort, and she the living image of Cooby. Soon the cow came out, and with her a girl with a pail and spancel.

"Oh, then," said Mrs. Connors, "I'd swear that is Cooby, only that we are after eating the most of her. She has the white spots on her back and the horns growing into her eyes."

The girl milked the cow, and then cow and girl disappeared. Mrs. Connors meant to tell her husband that night about the cow, but she forgot it, they having no meat for supper.

The following day Tom went again to cut turf, the woman went to milk, and again she saw the cow go into the fort, and the girl come out with a pail and a spancel. The girl tied the cow's legs, and sitting under her began to milk.

"God knows 'tis the very cow, and sure why shouldn't I know Cooby with the three white spots and the bent horns," thought Mrs. Connors, and she watched the cow and girl till the milking was over and thought, "I'll tell Tom to-night, and he may do what he likes, but I'll have nothing to do with fort or fairies myself."

When Connors came home in the evening, the first words before him were: "Wisha then, Tom, I have the news for you to-night."

"And what news is it?" asked Tom.

"You remember Cooby?"

"Why shouldn't I remember Cooby, and we after eating the most of her?"

"Indeed then, Tom, I saw Cooby to-day, and she inside in the fort and a girl milking her."

"Don't be making a fool of yourself. Is it the cow we are eating that would be in the fort giving milk?"

"Faith, then, I saw her and the three white spots on her back."

"But what is the use in telling me the like of that," said Tom, "when we haven't but two or three bits of her left inside in the tub?"

"If we haven't itself, I saw Cooby to-day."

"Well, I'll go in the morning, and if it's our Cooby that's in it I'll bring her home with me," said Tom, "if all the devils in the fort were before me."

"Ah, Tom, if it's to the fort you'll be going, don't forget to put holy water over you before you go."

Early in the morning Tom started across his land, and never stopped till he came to the fort, and there, sure enough, he saw the cow walking in through the gap to the fort, and he knew her that minute.

"'Tis my cow Cooby," said Connors, "and I'll have her. I'd like to see the man would keep her from me."

That minute the girl came out with her pail and spancel and was going up to Cooby.

"Stop where you are; don't milk that cow!" cried Connors, and springing toward the cow he caught her by the horn. "Let go the cow," said Tom; "this is my cow. It's a year that she's from me now. Go to your master and tell him to come out to me."

The girl went inside the fort and disappeared; but soon a fine-looking young man came and spoke to Connors. "What are you doing here, my man," asked he, "and why did you stop my servant from milking the cow?"

"She is my cow," said Tom, "and by that same token I'll keep her; and that's why I stopped the girl from milking her."

"How could she be your cow? Haven't I this cow a long time, and aren't you after eating your own cow?"

"I don't care what cow I'm after eating," said Tom. "I'll have this cow, for she is my Cooby."

They argued and argued. Tom declared that he'd take the cow home. "And if you try to prevent me," said he to the man, "I'll tear the fort to pieces or take her with me."

"Indeed, then, you'll not tear the fort."

Tom got so vexed that he made at the man. The man ran and Tom after him into the fort. When Tom was inside he forgot all about fighting. He saw many people dancing and enjoying themselves, and he thought, "Why shouldn't I do the like myself?" With that he made up to a fine-looking girl, and, taking her out to dance, told the piper to strike up a hornpipe, and he did.

Tom danced till he was tired. He offered twopence to the piper, but not a penny would the piper take from him.

The young man came up and said, "Well, you are a brave man and courageous, and for the future we'll be good friends. You can take the cow."

"I will not take her; you may keep her and welcome, for you are all very good people."

"Well," said the young man, "the cow is yours, and it's why I took her because there were many children in the fort without nurses, but the children are reared now, and you may take the cow. I put an old stray horse in place of her and made him look like your own beast, and it's an old horse you're eating all the year. From this out you'll grow rich and have luck. We'll not trouble you, but help you."

Tom took the cow and drove her home. From that out Tom Connors's cows had two calves apiece and his mare had two foals and his sheep two lambs every year, and every acre of the land he had gave him as much crop in one year as another man got from an acre in seven. At last Connors was a very rich man; and why not, when the fairies were with him?

THE BREWERY of EGG-SHELLS

Ireland

Mrs. Sullivan fancied that her youngest child had been exchanged by "fairies theft," and certainly appearances warranted such a conclusion; for in one night her healthy, blue-eyed boy had become shrivelled up into almost nothing, and never ceased squalling and crying. This naturally made poor Mrs. Sullivan very unhappy; and all the neighbours, by way of comforting her, said that her own child was, beyond any kind of doubt, with the good people, and that one of themselves was put in his place.

Mrs. Sullivan of course could not disbelieve what every one told her, but she did not wish to hurt the thing; for although its face was so withered, and its body wasted away to a mere skeleton, it had still a strong resemblance to her own boy. She, therefore, could not find it in her heart to roast it alive on the griddle, or to burn its nose off with the red-hot tongs, or to throw it out in the snow on the road-side, notwithstanding these, and several like proceedings, were strongly recommended to her for the recovery of her child.

One day who should Mrs. Sullivan meet but a cunning woman, well known about the country by the name of Ellen Leah (or Grey Ellen). She had the gift, however she got it, of telling where the dead were, and what was good for the rest of their souls; and could charm away warts and wens, and do a great many wonderful things of the same nature.

"You're in grief this morning, Mrs. Sullivan," were the first words of Ellen Leah to her.

"You may say that, Ellen," said Mrs. Sullivan, "and good cause I have to be in grief, for there was my own fine child whipped off from me out of his cradle, without as much as 'by your leave' or 'ask your pardon,' and an ugly dony bit of a shrivelled-up fairy put in his place; no wonder, then, that you see me in grief, Ellen."

"Small blame to you, Mrs. Sullivan," said Ellen Leah, "but are you sure 'tis a fairy?"

"Sure!" echoed Mrs. Sullivan, "sure enough I am to my sorrow, and can I doubt my own two eyes? Every mother's soul must feel for me!"

"Will you take an old woman's advice?" said Ellen Leah, fixing her wild and mysterious gaze upon the unhappy mother; and, after a pause, she added, "but maybe you'll call it foolish?"

"Can you get me back my child, my own child, Ellen?" said Mrs. Sullivan with great energy.

"If you do as I bid you," returned Ellen Leah, "you'll know." Mrs. Sullivan was silent in expectation, and Ellen continued, "Put down the big pot, full of water, on the fire, and make it boil like mad; then get a dozen new-laid eggs, break them, and keep the shells, but throw away the rest; when that is done, put the shells in the pot of boiling water, and you will soon know whether it is your own boy or a fairy. If you find that it is a fairy in the cradle, take the red-hot poker and cram it down his ugly throat, and you will not have much trouble with him after that, I promise you."

Home went Mrs. Sullivan, and did as Ellen Leah desired. She put the pot on the fire, and plenty of turf under it, and set the water boiling at such a rate, that if ever water was red-hot, it surely was.

The child was lying, for a wonder, quite easy and quiet in the cradle, every now and then cocking his eye, that would twinkle as keen as a star in a frosty night, over at the great fire, and the big pot upon it; and he looked on with great attention at Mrs. Sullivan breaking the eggs and putting down the egg-shells to boil. At last he asked, with the voice of a very old man, "What are you doing, mammy?"

Mrs. Sullivan's heart, as she said herself, was up in her mouth ready to choke her, at hearing the child speak. But she contrived to put the poker in the fire, and to answer, without making any wonder at the words, "I'm brewing, *a vick.*"[1]

---

1. my son

"And what are you brewing, mammy?" said the little imp, whose supernatural gift of speech now proved beyond question that he was a fairy substitute.

"I wish the poker was red," thought Mrs. Sullivan; but it was a large one, and took a long time heating; so she determined to keep him in talk until the poker was in a proper state to thrust down his throat, and therefore repeated the question.

"Is it what I'm brewing, *a vick*," said she, "you want to know?"

"Yes, mammy: what are you brewing?" returned the fairy.

"Egg-shells, *a vick*," said Mrs. Sullivan.

"Oh!" shrieked the imp, starting up in the cradle, and clapping his hands together, "I'm fifteen hundred years in the world, and I never saw a brewery of egg-shells before!" The poker was by this time quite red, and Mrs. Sullivan, seizing it, ran furiously towards the cradle; but somehow or other her foot slipped, and she fell flat on the floor, and the poker flew out of her hand to the other end of the house. However, she got up without much loss of time and went to the cradle, intending to pitch the wicked thing that was in it into the pot of boiling water, when there she saw her own child in a sweet sleep, one of his soft round arms rested upon the pillow—his features were as placid as if their repose had never been disturbed, save the rosy mouth, which moved with a gentle and regular breathing.

THE FAIRIES of RAHONAIN and ELIZABETH SHEA

Ireland

About thirty years ago, said the old man, there lived in a village near Rahonain Castle a man named James Kivane, a step-brother of my own, and he married a woman called Elizabeth Shea. Three or four nights after her second child was born Kivane's wife, who was attended by her own mother and her mother-in-law, woke and saw the bed on fire. She called to the mother, who was there at the bedside, but had fallen asleep. The mother sprang up, and, turning towards the hearth, saw a cat with the face of a man on her, and was frightened, but she had no time to look longer at the cat. When she had the fire quenched she looked for the cat, but not a trace of her could they find in the house, and they never caught a sight of her again.

Two days later the young child died, and three or four days after that the woman had a terrible pain in her foot. It swelled to a great size, and where the swelling was the skin looked like the bark of a tree. The poor woman suffered terribly. They sent for the priest many times, and spent money for masses. They offered one priest twenty pounds to cure her, but he said that if all the money in the kingdom were offered he would have nothing to do with the case. He was afraid of getting a fairy stroke himself.

The foot was swelling always, and it was that size that a yard of linen was needed to go once around it. The woman was a year and a half in this way, and towards the end she said that horses and carriages were moving around the house every night, but she had no knowledge of why they were in it.

The mother went to an old woman, an herb doctor, and begged her to come and cure her daughter if she could.

"I can cure her," said the woman, "but if I do you must let some other one of your family go in place of her."

Now, as all the sons and daughters were married and had families of their own, the mother said she had no one she could put in place of this daughter. Kivane's wife used to raise herself by a rope which was put hanging above the bed. When tired and she could hold no longer, she would lie down again. The woman remained in suffering like this till a week before she died. She told her friends that it was no use to give her remedies or pay money for masses to benefit her; that it wasn't herself that was in it at all.

On the night that the mother saw the cat with a man's face and she sitting on the hearth, Kivane's real wife was taken by the fairies and put in Rahonain Castle to nurse a young child.

Nobody could tell who the sick woman was, but whoever she was she died, and the body was so swollen and drawn up that the coffin was like a great box, as broad as 'twas long. About a year after the funeral Pat Mahony, who worked for a hotel-keeper in Dingle, went to a fair at Listowel. At the fair a strange man came up to Mahony. "Where do you live?" asked the man.

"In Dingle," said Pat Mahony.

"Do you know families at Rahonain named Shea and Kivane?"

"I do," said Mahony. "Kivane's wife died about a twelvemonth ago."

"Well," said the strange man, "I have a message for you to the parents of that woman, Elizabeth Shea. She is coming to my house for the last nine months. She comes always after sunset. She lives in a fairy fort that is on my land. This is the way we discovered the woman: About nine months ago potatoes and milk were put out on the dresser for one of my servants who was away from home, and before the man came this woman was seen going to the dresser and eating the potatoes and drinking the milk. She came every evening after that for about a month before I had courage to speak to her. When I spoke she told me that her father, mother, husband, and child were living near Rahonain Castle, She gave every right token of who she was. 'I spent,' said she, 'three months in Rahonain, at first nursing a child that was in it, but was taken after that to the fort on the place where I am living now, in Lismore. I have not tasted food in the fort yet,' said she, 'but at the end of seven years I'll be forced to eat and drink unless somebody saves me; I cannot escape unassisted.'"

When Mahony came home to Dingle he went straight to Rahonain and told the woman's friends all that the strange man had told him. She had told the man, too, how her friends must come with four men and a horse and cart; that she would meet them.

Mrs. Kivane's father and brother, and I and another neighbouring man, offered to go to Lismore, but Kivane wouldn't go, for he had a second wife at this time. The following morning we started, and went to the parish priest to take his advice. He told us not to go, and advised us in every way to stay at home. He was afraid, I suppose, that the woman might give the people too much knowledge of the other world. The other three men were stopped by the priest. Sure there was no use in my going alone, and I didn't.

Kivane's wife knew that her husband was married the second time, for she sent word to him that she didn't care, she would live with her father and her child. Everybody forgot the affair for a couple of years. When a retired policeman named Bat O'Connor was going from Lismore to Dingle, the woman appeared before him, saluted him, and asked was he going to Dingle, and he said he was. She told him then if he wanted to do her any good or service to go to her friends at Rahonain (she gave their names) and tell them that they had plenty of time yet to go and claim her; that she had not eaten fairy food so far. He promised to do as she asked. He reached Dingle soon after, went to Rahonain and told her friends what she had said. O'Connor, however, didn't tell everything in full till they would promise to go. At this the relations of Kivane's second wife went to O'Connor and bribed him to say nothing more. After that he was silent, and people cared no more about the woman.

The seven years passed, and at the end of that time Elizabeth Shea's father saw her one evening when he was coming home from market and was about a mile beyond Dingle. She walked nearly a mile with him, but didn't talk. At parting she gave him a blow on the face. On the following day he had to take to his bed, and was blind for seven or eight years. He kept the bed most of the time till he died. During the couple of days before he lost his sight Shea saw the daughter come in and give a blow to her child, which died strangely soon after. Neither priest nor doctor could tell what ailment was on the child.

About the time the child died Kivane's second wife got sick, and has not milked a cow nor swept the house since. She has not gone to mass or market these twenty years. She keeps the bed now, and will keep it while she lives. She has no pain and is not suffering in any way, but is dead in herself, as it were. She had a fine young girl of a daughter, but she got a blow and died two days after. She has three sons, but Elizabeth Shea has never done them any harm.

LESSONS LEARNED

WHIPPETY-STOURIE

Scotland

I am going to tell you a story about a poor young widow woman, who lived in a house called Kittlerumpit, though whereabouts in Scotland the house of Kittlerumpit stood nobody knows.

Some folk think that it stood in the neighbourhood of the Debateable Land, which, as all the world knows, was on the Borders, where the old Border Reivers were constantly coming and going; the Scotch stealing from the English, and the English from the Scotch. Be that as it may, the widowed Mistress of Kittlerumpit was sorely to be pitied.

For she had lost her husband, and no one quite knew what had become of him. He had gone to a fair one day, and had never come back again, and although everybody believed that he was dead, no one knew how he died.

Some people said that he had been persuaded to enlist, and had been killed in the wars; others, that he had been taken away to serve as a sailor by the press-gang, and had been drowned at sea.

At any rate, his poor young wife was sorely to be pitied, for she was left with a little baby-boy to bring up, and, as times were bad, she had not much to live on.

But she loved her baby dearly, and worked all day amongst her cows, and pigs, and hens, in order to earn enough money to buy food and clothes for both herself and him.

Now, on the morning of which I am speaking, she rose very early and went out to feed her pigs, for rent-day was coming on, and she intended to take one of them, a great, big, fat creature, to the market that very day, as she thought that the price that it would fetch would go a long way towards paying her rent.

And because she thought so, her heart was light, and she hummed a little song to herself as she crossed the yard with her bucket on one arm and her baby-boy on the other.

But the song was quickly changed into a cry of despair when she reached the pig-sty, for there lay her cherished pig on its back, with its legs in the air and its eyes shut, just as if it were going to breathe its last breath.

"What shall I do? What shall I do?" cried the poor woman, sitting down on a big stone and clasping her boy to her breast, heedless of the fact that she had dropped her bucket, and that the pig's-meat was running out, and that the hens were eating it.

"First I lost my husband, and now I am going to lose my finest pig. The pig that I hoped would fetch a deal of money."

Now I must explain to you that the house of Kittlerumpit stood on a hillside, with a great fir wood behind it, and the ground sloping down steeply in front.

And as the poor young thing, after having a good cry to herself, was drying her eyes, she chanced to look down the hill, and who should she see coming up it but an Old Woman, who looked like a lady born.

She was dressed all in green, with a white apron, and she wore a black velvet hood on her head, and a steeple-crowned beaver hat over that, something like those, as I have heard tell, that the women wear in Wales. She walked very slowly, leaning on a long staff, and she gave a bit of a hirple now and then, as if she were lame.

As she drew near, the young widow felt it was becoming to rise and curtsey to the Gentlewoman, for such she saw her to be.

"Madam," she said, with a sob in her voice, "I bid you welcome to the house of Kittlerumpit, although you find its Mistress one of the most unfortunate women in the world."

"Hout-tout," answered the Old Lady, in such a harsh voice that the young woman started, and grasped her baby tighter in her arms. "Ye have little need to say that. Ye have lost your husband, I grant ye, but there were worse losses at

Shirra-Muir. And now your pig is like to die—I could, maybe, remedy that. But I must first hear how much ye would give me if I cured him."

"Anything that your Ladyship's Madam likes to ask," replied the widow, too much delighted at having the animal's life saved to think that she was making rather a rash promise.

"Very good," said the old Dame, and without wasting any more words she walked straight into the pig-sty.

She stood and looked at the dying creature for some minutes, rocking to and fro and muttering to herself in words which the widow could not understand; at least, she could only understand four of them, and they sounded something like this:

"Pitter-patter,
Haly water."

Then she put her hand into her pocket and drew out a tiny bottle with a liquid that looked like oil in it. She took the cork out, and dropped one of her long lady-like fingers into it; then she touched the pig on the snout and on his ears, and on the tip of his curly tail.

No sooner had she done so than up the beast jumped, and, with a grunt of contentment, ran off to its trough to look for its breakfast.

A joyful woman was the Mistress of Kittlerumpit when she saw it do this, for she felt that her rent was safe; and in her relief and gratitude she would have kissed the hem of the strange Lady's green gown, if she would have allowed it, but she would not.

"No, no," said she, and her voice sounded harsher than ever. "Let us have no fine meanderings, but let us stick to our bargain. I have done my part, and mended the pig; now ye must do yours, and give me what I like to ask—your son."

Then the poor widow gave a piteous cry, for she knew now what she had not guessed before—that the Green-clad Lady was a Fairy, and a Wicked Fairy too, else had she not asked such a terrible thing.

It was too late now, however, to pray, and beseech, and beg for mercy; the Fairy stood her ground, hard and cruel.

"Ye promised me what I liked to ask, and I have asked your son; and your son I will have," she replied, "so it is useless making such a din about it. But one thing I may tell you, for I know well that the knowledge will not help you. By the laws of Fairy-land, I cannot take the bairn till the third day after this, and if by that time you have found out my name I cannot take him even then. But ye will not be able to find it out, of that I am certain. So I will call back for the boy in three days."

And with that she disappeared round the back of the pig-sty, and the poor mother fell down in a dead faint beside the stone.

All that day, and all the next, she did nothing but sit in her kitchen and cry, and hug her baby tighter in her arms; but on the day before that on which the Fairy said that she was coming back, she felt as if she must get a little breath of fresh air, so she went for a walk in the fir wood behind the house.

Now in this fir wood there was an old quarry hole, in the bottom of which was a bonnie spring well, the water of which was always sweet and pure. The young widow was walking near this quarry hole, when, to her astonishment, she heard the whirr of a spinning-wheel and the sound of a voice lilting a song. At first she could not think where the sound came from; then, remembering the quarry, she laid down her child at a tree root, and crept noiselessly through the bushes on her hands and knees to the edge of the hole and peeped over.

She could hardly believe her eyes! For there, far below her, at the bottom of the quarry, beside the spring well, sat the cruel Fairy, dressed in her green frock and tall felt hat, spinning away as fast as she could at a tiny spinning-wheel.

And what should she be singing but—

> "Little kens our guid dame at hame,[1]
> Whippety-Stourie is my name."

The widow woman almost cried aloud for joy, for now she had learned the Fairy's secret, and her child was safe. But she dare not, in case the wicked old Dame heard her and threw some other spell over her.

---

1. Little does the good woman at home know

So she crept softly back to the place where she had left her child; then, catching him up in her arms, she ran through the wood to her house, laughing, and singing, and tossing him in the air in such a state of delight that, if anyone had met her, they would have been in danger of thinking that she was mad.

Now this young woman had been a merry-hearted maiden, and would have been merry-hearted still, if, since her marriage, she had not had so much trouble that it had made her grow old and sober-minded before her time; and she began to think what fun it would be to tease the Fairy for a few minutes before she let her know that she had found out her name.

So next day, at the appointed time, she went out with her boy in her arms, and seated herself on the big stone where she had sat before; and when she saw the old Dame coming up the hill, she crumpled up her nice clean cap, and screwed up her face, and pretended to be in great distress and to be crying bitterly.

The Fairy took no notice of this, however, but came close up to her, and said, in her harsh, merciless voice, "Good wife of Kittlerumpit, ye ken the reason of my coming; give me the bairn."

Then the young mother pretended to be in sorer distress than ever, and fell on her knees before the wicked old woman and begged for mercy.

"Oh, sweet Madam Mistress," she cried, "spare me my bairn, and take, an' thou wilt, the pig instead."

"We have no need of bacon where I come from," answered the Fairy coldly; "so give me the laddie and let me begone—I have no time to waste in this wise."

"Oh, dear Lady mine," pleaded the Goodwife, "if thou wilt not have the pig, wilt thou not spare my poor bairn and take me myself?"

The Fairy stepped back a little, as if in astonishment. "Art thou mad, woman," she cried contemptuously, "that thou proposest such a thing? Who in all the world would care to take a plain-looking, red-eyed, dowdy wife like thee with them?"

Now the young Mistress of Kittlerumpit knew that she was no beauty, and the knowledge had never vexed her; but something in the Fairy's tone made her feel so angry that she could contain herself no longer.

"In troth, fair Madam, I might have had the wit to know that the like of me is not fit to tie the shoe-string of the High and Mighty Princess, WHIPPETY-STOURIE!"

If there had been a charge of gunpowder buried in the ground, and if it had suddenly exploded beneath her feet, the Wicked Fairy could not have jumped higher into the air.

And when she came down again she simply turned round and ran down the brae, shrieking with rage and disappointment, for all the world, as an old book says, "like an owl chased by witches."

AN ORKNEY SELKIE STORY

Scotland

The goodman of Wastness was well-to-do, had his farm well stocked, and was a good-looking and well-favoured man. And though many braw lasses in the island had set their caps at him, he was not to be caught. So the young lasses began to treat him with contempt, regarding him as an old young man who was deliberately committing the unpardonable sin of celibacy. He did not trouble his head much about the lasses, and when urged by his friends to take a wife, he said, "Women were like many another thing in this weary world, only sent for a trial to man; and I have trials enough without being tried by a wife. If that old fool Adam had not been bewitched by his wife, he might have been a happy man in the yard of Eden to this day." The old wife of Longer, who heard him make this speech, said to him, "Take due heed of yourself, you'll maybe yourself be bewitched some day." "Ay," quoth he, "that will be when you walk dry shod from the Alters of Seenie to the Boar of Papa."

Well, it happened one day that the goodman of Wastness was down on the ebb,[1] when he saw at a little distance a number of selkie folk on a flat rock. Some were lying sunning themselves, while others jumped and played about in great glee. They were all naked, and had skins as white as his own. The rock on which they sported had deep water on its seaward side, and on its shore side a shallow pool. The goodman of Wastness crept unseen till he got to the edge of the shallow

1. that portion of the shore left dry at low water

pool; he then rose and dashed through the pool to the rock on its other side. The alarmed selkie folk seized their seal skins, and, in mad haste, jumped into the sea. Quick as they were, the goodman was also quick, and he seized one of the skins belonging to an unfortunate damsel, who in terror of flight neglected to clutch it as she sprang into the water.

The selkie folk swam out a little distance, then turning, set up their heads and gazed at the goodman. He noticed that one of them had not the appearance of seals like the rest. He then took the captured skin under his arm, and made for home, but before he got out of the ebb, he heard a most doleful sound of weeping and lamentation behind him. He turned to see a fair woman following him. It was that one of the selkie folk whose seal skin he had taken. She was a pitiful sight; sobbing in bitter grief, holding out both hands in eager supplication, while the big tears followed each other down her fair face. And ever and anon she cried out, "O bonnie man! If there's only mercy in your human breast, give back my skin! I cannot, cannot, cannot live in the sea without it. I cannot, cannot, cannot bide among my own folk without my own seal skin. Oh, pity a poor distressed, forlorn lass, if you would ever hope for mercy yourself!" The goodman was not too soft-hearted, yet he could not help pitying her in her doleful plight. And with his pity came the softer passion of love. His heart that never loved women before was conquered by the sea-nymph's beauty. So, after a great deal of higgling and plenty of love-making, he wrung from the sea-lass a reluctant consent to live with him as his wife. She chose this as the least of two evils. Without the skin she could not live in the sea, and he absolutely refused to give up the skin.

So the sea-lass went with the goodman and stayed with him for many days, being a thrifty, frugal, and kindly goodwife.

She bore her goodman seven children, four boys and three lasses, and there were not bonnier lasses or statelier boys in all the isle. And though the goodwife of Wastness appeared happy, and was sometimes merry, yet there seemed at times to be a weight on her heart; and many a long longing look did she fix on the sea. She taught her bairns many a strange song, that nobody on earth ever heard before. Albeit she was a thing of the sea, yet the goodman led a happy life with her.

Now it chanced, one fine day, that the goodman of Wastness and his three eldest sons were off in his boat to the fishing. Then the goodwife sent three of the other children to the ebb to gather limpits and wilks. The youngest lass had to stay at home, for she had a beelan[2] foot. The goodwife then began, under the pretence of house-cleaning, a determined search for her long-lost skin. She searched up, and she search down; she searched but, and she searched ben; she searched out, and she searched in, but never a skin could she find, while the sun wore to the west. The youngest lass sat in a stool with her sore foot on a cringlo.[3] Says she to her mother, "Mam, what are you looking for?" "O bairn, do not tell," said her mother, "but I'm looking for a bonnie skin, to make a rivlin[4] that would cure your sore foot." Says the lass, "Maybe I know where it is. One day, when you were all out, and Daddy thought I was sleepin' in the bed, he took a bonnie skin down; he glowered at it a short minute, then folded it and laid it up under the aisins[5] above the bed."

When her mother heard this she rushed to the place, and pulled out her long-concealed skin. "Farewell, little buddo!"[6] said she to the child, and ran out. She rushed to the shore, flung on her skin, and plunged into the sea with a wild cry of joy. A male of the selkie folk there met and greeted her with every token of delight. The goodman was rowing home, and saw them both from his boat. His lost wife uncovered her face, and thus she cried to him: "Goodman of Wastness, farewell to you! I liked you well, you were good to me; but I love better my man of the sea!" And that was the last he ever saw or heard of his bonnie wife. Often did he wander on the sea-shore, hoping to meet his lost love, but never more saw he her fair face.

---

2. suppurating
3. a low straw stool
4. shoe or sandal
5. space left by slope of roof over wall-head when not beam-filled
6. a term of endearment

THE WHITE TROUT

Ireland

There was once upon a time, long ago, a beautiful lady that lived in a castle upon the lake beyond, and they say she was promised to a king's son, and they were to be married, when all of a sudden he was murdered, the creature (Lord help us), and thrown into the lake above, and so, of course, he couldn't keep his promise to the fair lady,—and more's the pity.

Well, the story goes that she went out of her mind, because of losing the king's son—for she was tender-hearted, God help her, like the rest of us!—and pined away after him, until at last, no one about seen her, good or bad; and the story went that the fairies took her away.

Well, sir, in course of time, the White Trout, God bless it, was seen in the stream beyond, and sure the people didn't know what to think of the creature, seeing as how a *white* trout was never heard of afor, nor since; and years upon years the trout was there, just where you seen it this blessed minute, longer nor I can tell—aye throth, and beyond the memory of the oldest in the village.

At last the people began to think it must be a fairy; for what else could it be?—and no hurt nor harm was ever put on the white trout, until some wicked sinners of soldiers came to these parts, and laughed at all the people, and gibed and jeered them for thinking of the likes; and one of them in particular (bad luck to him; God forgive me for saying it!) swore he'd catch the trout and eat it for his dinner—the blackguard!

Well, what would you think of the villainy of the soldier? Sure enough he caught the trout, and away with him home, and puts on the frying-pan, and into it he pitches the purty little thing. The throut squeeled all as one as a Christian creature, and, my dear, you'd think the soldier would split his sides laughing—for he was a hardened villain; and when he thought one side was done, he turns it over to fry the other; and, what would you think, but the devil a taste of a burn was on it at all at all; and sure the soldier thought it was a *queer* trout that could not be broiled. "But," says he, "I'll give it another turn by-and-by," little thinking what was in store for him, the heathen.

Well, when he thought that side was done he turns it again, and lo and behold you, the devil a taste more done that side was nor the other. "Bad luck to me," says the soldier, "but that beats the world," says he; "but I'll fry you again, my darling," says he, "as cunning as you think yourself;" and so with that he turns it over and over, but not a sign of the fire was on the purty trout. "Well," says the desperate villain—(for sure, sir, only he was a desperate villain *entirely*, he might know he was doing a wrong thing, seeing that all his endeavors was no good)—"Well," says he, "my jolly little trout, maybe you're fried enough, though you don't seem over well dressed; but you may be better than you look, like a singed cat, and a tid-bit after all," says he; and with that he ups with his knife and fork to taste a piece of the trout; but, my jewel, the minute he puts his knife into the fish, there was a murdering screech, that you'd think the life would leave you if you heard it, and away jumps the trout out of the frying-pan into the middle of the floor; and on the spot where it fell, up rose a lovely lady—the beautifullest creature that eyes ever seen, dressed in white, and a band of gold in her hair, and a stream of blood running down her arm.

"Look where you cut me, you villain," says she, and she held out her arm to him—and, my dear, he thought the sight would leave his eyes.

"Couldn't you leave me cool and comfortable in the river where you snared me, and not disturb me in my duty?" says she.

Well, he trembled like a dog in a wet sack, and at last he stammered out something, and begged for his life, and asked her ladyship's pardon, and said he didn't know she was on duty, or he was too good a soldier not to know better nor to meddle with her.

"I *was* on duty, then," says the lady; "I was watching for my true love that is coming by water to me," says she, "and if he comes while I'm away, and that I miss of him, I'll turn you into a pinkeen, and I'll hunt you up and down for evermore, while grass grows or water runs."

Well, the soldier thought the life would leave him, at the thoughts of his being turned into a pinkeen, and begged for mercy; and with that says the lady—

"Renounce your evil courses," says she, "you villain, or you'll repent it too late; be a good man for the future, and go to your duty[1] regular, and now," says she, "take me back and put me into the river again, where you found me."

"Oh, my lady," says the soldier, "how could I have the heart to drown a beautiful lady like you?"

But before he could say another word, the lady was vanished, and there he saw the little trout on the ground. Well he put it in a clean plate, and away he runs for the bare life, for fear her lover would come while she was away; and he run, and he run, even till he came to the cave again, and threw the trout into the river. The minute he did, the water was as red as blood for a little while, by reason of the cut, I suppose, until the stream washed the stain away; and to this day there's a little red mark on the trout's side, where it was cut.[2]

Well, sir, from that day out the soldier was an altered man, and reformed his ways, and went to his duty regular, and fasted three times a-week—though it was never fish he took on fasting days, for after the fright he got, fish would never rest on his stomach—saving your presence.

But anyhow, he was an altered man, as I said before, and in course of time he left the army, and turned hermit at last; and they say he used to pray evermore for the soul of the White Trout.

---

1. The Irish peasant calls his attendance at the confessional "going to his duty."
2. The fish has really a red spot on its side.

THE FOUR GIFTS

Brittany

If I had three hundred crowns a year, I should go and live at Quimper, where is the finest church in all Cornouailles and where all the houses have weather-cocks; if I had two hundred crowns a year, I should go and live at Carhaix, for its moorlands and game, but if I had only one hundred crowns, I should settle down at Pont-Aven, for it is there you find an abundance of everything. At Pont-Aven, butter costs but the price of milk at Quimper, a fowl what you pay for a Quimper egg. That is why at Pont-Aven you see fine farms, where you have home-cured bacon three times a week and even shepherd-lads have as much homemade bread as they can eat.

It was in one of such estates that Azénor Bourhis lived; she toiled from dawn till night, keeping her farm as though she had been born a man, and owning fields and produce enough to pay for two sons' schooling. But in place of sons Azénor had one niece who earned more than her keep, so that each day's savings were added to the day's before. Thus the old dame's purse grew fat before her very eyes.

Now, savings too easily earned bring evil in their train. If you store up corn, rats come into the barn, and if you hoard up crowns, miserliness grips the heart. Old Azénor had gotten to the point of caring only about wealth, and of esteeming people only like herself, who had plenty of money in their pockets. So she was angry when she saw Dénès, a farm laborer from Plover, having private talks with her niece.

One day when Azénor again had seen the two together she called to Téphany in a rasping tone:

"Are you not ashamed to be chattering with that beggar, when you can find many a rich lad hereabouts who would be glad to buy you a silver ring?"

"Dénès is a skillful farmer and as upright as the hills," replied the maiden. "One of these days he will find a farm to let, big enough to bring up little children on it."

"And you would like to be their mother?" burst out Azénor wrathfully. "By my purse strings! I would rather see you at the bottom of our well, than the wife of that good-for-nothing. No! No! No one shall say I have brought up my sister's child only to see her marry a man whose whole possessions could go into his tobacco-pouch!"

"What does money matter when you have health and the good saints know your intentions are of the best?" answered Téphany gently.

"What does money matter!" retorted Azénor, horrorstruck. "Do you then despise the goods that heaven gives us! Since it is so, you impertinent baggage, I forbid you to speak again to Dénès, and if I catch him on our lands I shall ask the Rector to blame you publicly on Sunday!"

"Oh! you would not truly do so!" cried Téphany quite terrified.

"As sure as there is a Paradise waiting for us all, I will!" flared back the angry dame. "In the meantime, away to the brook with you and wash the linen and put it to dry on the hawthorn hedge, for ever since you've listened to the wind that blows from Plover town, all your work has been forgotten, and both your arms are worth no more than a one-armed man's five fingers."

With which bitter words Azénor pointed to the scrubbing board and ordered Téphany to her task. The girl obeyed, but her heart was welling with grief and resentment.

"Crabbed age is harder than the stone stoop of our farm," she brooded. "Yes, a hundred times as hard, for the rain, falling drop by drop, wears away the stone but tears cannot soften old folks' stubbornness. Heaven knows my meetings with Dénès were my only joy. He never taught me anything but beautiful songs, and talked to me only about what we should do when we were married in our little farm,—he looking after the land, and the mangers. Is it wrong to give each other courage and hope? God would never have created marriage if it were a sin to think of one's own wedding! Ah! cruel, cruel aunt to tear me from my Dénès!"

So thinking, Téphany reached the brook. As she was putting down her tub of linen on the flat, white stones that marked the washing-place, she saw a wizened woman, not of that parish, who was leaning on a hawthorn wand. In spite of her trouble, Téphany greeted her, calling her "Aunt," according to the ways of Old Breton courtesy. Young folk had warm hearts in those days of long ago.

"Are you resting under the cool willow tree, Aunt?" she asked.

"You have to rest where best you may, when the sky is your only roof," replied the shrivelled woman in a quavery voice.

"Are you then so forlorn?" inquired Téphany pitifully, "and have you no relations to give you welcome in their home?"

"All have gone to heaven," continued the crone, "and my only home is kind hearts."

The maiden took the piece of homemade bread and the slice of bacon which Azénor had given her, wrapped up in a bit of clean linen, and offered it to the beggar woman. The dame had a hungry look.

"Take this, poor Aunt," said Téphany. "Today at least, with this good bread you will have a Christian dinner. In your prayers, remember my dear parents who have died."

The dame took the bread and peered at Téphany.

"Those who help are worthy to be helped," she remarked. "Your eyes are red because your aunt Azénor has forbidden you to talk to your lad from Plover,—but I shall give you the means of seeing him once a day."

"You will!" cried the girl, dumbfounded that this old dame should know so much about her.

"Take this brass pin," resumed the crone. "Each time you prick it into your collar Mother Bourhis will feel compelled to leave the farmhouse and go into the field to count her cabbages. As long as the pin is in its place you will be free and your aunt will come back only when the pin lies once more in its sheath."

Having pronounced these words, the beggar woman rose, waved her hand and disappeared.

Téphany stood thunderstruck. It was certain that the wrinkled dame had been a saint or fairy. The girl went home quite decided to try what the pin could do.

The next day at about the time that Dénès usually arrived Téphany placed the brass pin in her collar. Immediately Azénor took her wooden shoes and went out into the garden, where she fell to counting the cabbages. From the garden, she went to the orchard, from the orchard, to the other fields, so that the lassie had plenty of time to talk with the lad from Plover.

It was the same the next day, and every day for week following week. As soon as the pin came from its sheath, Téphany's aunt would trot off to her cabbages and begin to calculate again and yet again the number of the big ones, the little ones, the smooth ones or the curly. Who would not have a pin like this!

At first Dénès was delighted, but as week followed week he became less eager for his talks with Téphany. He had taught her all the songs he knew. He had gone over his plans again and again and now he was obliged to wonder what he was going to say to her, and to get it ready beforehand, as a preacher prepares his sermon. So he came later and went away earlier. At length days arrived when he did not come at all, and the waiting Téphany twiddled her pin in vain.

Alas, poor Téphany!

She felt her lover's heart becoming cold and she was sadder now than in the days before she had the magic pin.

There came an evening when Téphany, having waited uselessly for her beloved, took her pitcher and went alone to the spring, her heart heavy with sorrow. As she drew near, she beheld again the wizened woman, who had given her the pin. When the crone saw Téphany she began to laugh and addressed her in a squeaky voice:

"Ah! Ah! my fine lady does not care about being able to talk to her beloved Dénès at any time in the day?"

"Alas," sighed Téphany, "I had to see him to keep his heart in love with me, but now habit has made my society less pleasant. Ah! Aunt! since you gave me the means of seeing him every day, you ought to have given me the wit to hold him."

"Is that then what my lassie wants?" asked the aged woman. "So be it. Here is a feather. It comes from the wing of the oldest of the eagles, and no one knows how old he is. When my fair lady hides it in her hair, she will be as knowing as the will-o'-the-wisp himself."

Téphany, blushing with pleasure, took the feather and the next day, before Dénès' visit, she slipped it under the blue ribbon of her coif. It seemed instantly as if the sun had risen in her mind. She found knowledge that men take all of a lifetime to acquire was hers. A wealth, too, of other matters filled her brain which learned men know not at all. For to man's wisdom was added woman's wit. So Dénès was astonished at her flow of knowledge; she invented poetry and knew more songs than all the singers of Scaër, and repeated all the gossip of the neighborhood that on baking-days was going round from house to house.

The young man came back the next day and the days that followed, and Téphany had always something fresh to tell him. Dénès had never met a man nor woman half so witty, but it was not long before he felt himself a bit uneasy in his mind. Téphany could not help wearing her feather for other folk as well as Dénès and all over the countryside tongues began to wag about her songs and clever speeches.

"She's a bad lot," folk said of her. "The man who marries her will be led along for all the world like a bridled horse."

The lad from Plover began repeating the same prediction to himself, and as he had always thought it better to hold the bridle than to wear it, Téphany's jokes no longer made him laugh so heartily.

One day when he was going to a dance on a new threshing floor, the girl did her brightest to prevent him, but Dénès, who did not intend to be directed by her, would not listen to her reasons and laughed at her request.

"Ah! I see why you are so anxious to go to the new threshing floor," explained Téphany in a temper. "Azilicz will be there."

Azilicz was the prettiest girl in all the countryside and, as even all her best friends said, the vainest.

"It is certain Azilicz will be there," said Dénès, who was pleased to make his best-beloved jealous, "and a man would go a wearier way than that to see a maid so winsome."

"Then go where your heart bids you," cried Téphany, and she flounced into the farmhouse without listening to another word.

She sat down upon the hearthstone, overwhelmed with grief, and, tearing from her hair her magic feather, sobbed aloud with bitterness.

"Of what use is wit since men turn toward beauty as flies turn toward the sun! Ah! old fairy Aunt, what I needed was not to be the most learned, but the most beautiful of damsels."

"Then be the most beautiful," replied a voice close to her ear.

Téphany turned breathless, and behold! beside her stood the wrinkled crone with the hawthorn wand. The dame went on: "Take this necklace, and while you have it round your neck you will be to other women as the queen of flowers is to the wild blossoms of the meadows." Truly here was a necklace indeed!

Téphany uttered a cry of joy. She quickly donned the necklace, hastened to her looking-glass and gasped delighted. Never had been seen in all the land of Brittany a maid so flowerlike as she.

She determined to test immediately her beauty upon Dénès so, putting on her richest costume, her woollen stockings and buckled shoes, she set out for the threshing floor. When she reached the cross-roads, she met a young lord in a coach.

"By our Lady," he cried, leaping out beside her, "I did not know there was such a lovely creature in all the four corners of the land, and if I lose my soul for it, you shall bear my name."

But Téphany replied:

"Go your way, my lord, go your way; I am only a poor peasant girl, used to winnowing, milking, and harvesting."

"And I will make a lady of you!" exclaimed the lord, seizing her hand and drawing her toward his coach.

The girl drew back.

"I want only to be betrothed to Dénès, the ploughman of Plover," she cried, alarmed. But the young lord laughed. He ordered his servants to lay hands on Téphany and to lift her into his coach, which done they drove away as quickly as the horses could gallop. Amidst clouds of dust and a clattering of hoofs they reached the young lord's castle, which was of rock, roofed with slate, as are all the great nobles' houses. Her captor imprisoned Téphany in a vast and vaulted room, closed it with three bolted doors and placed guards to keep watch upon her. But scarcely had the young lord withdrawn than Téphany with sudden inspiration drew forth her pin of brass. At once her watchers hastened to the garden to count the cabbages. She then placed the feather in her hair and with her wits discovered, hidden in the panelling, a fourth door through which she fled. Soon she gained the brushwood through which she plunged as a wild creature that hears the hounds hot in pursuit. She panted on until night began to fall, then she found herself beside a convent at whose grated door she knocked and asked for shelter. The doorkeeper, when she beheld Téphany, shook her head.

"Nay, nay," she growled out surlily, "this is no place for smartly dressed girls who go about alone at night." And she clapped the door shut and dropped the clanging bolts into place.

Téphany stumbled on and on and came at length to a farm where lights were twinkling. Here again she stopped to ask for succor. At the door a boisterous group of farm-lads greeted her. They all cried out at Téphany's dazzling beauty, each one demanding that he have her for his wife. This quickly led to quarrelling, and the quarrelling in turn to fighting, so that frightened Téphany turned to flee. But all the lads ran after her. Suddenly remembering her necklace, she snatched it from her neck and threw it on a sow. At once the spell was broken that drew the lads to her. Her pursuers now pursued the pig, which grunted off in terror, and all vanished in the dark.

Téphany stumbled on her way and at last, footsore and sad at heart, she reached her aunt Azénor's farm.

So fraught with danger and with hardship had been the gift of beauty that Téphany found herself once more forming wishes. "Heaven forgive me!" she whispered to herself, "what I ought to have asked for, was neither the liberty of seeing Dénès every day, for he wearies of it, nor a sharp wit, for it frightens him away, nor beauty, for it brings troubles and distrust; I ought to have asked for wealth, which makes you master of yourself and all the world beside. Ah! if I dared ask the fairy for one thing more, I should be wiser than I was before!"

"Take your heart's wish," said the beggar woman's voice at Téphany's ear. "If you feel in your right-hand pocket, you will find a silver box. Rub your eyes with the pomade and you will have a treasure in yourself."

The girl felt quickly in her pocket, found the box, opened it and had just begun to rub her eyes, when Azénor Bourhis suddenly appeared.

For some time past, Azénor had lost long days in counting cabbages, and as she saw all work behindhand in the farm, she was on the watch for someone on whom to vent her temper. When she beheld her niece sitting idle, she exploded in a burst of wrath:

"Aha, and that's the way you work, while I am slaving in the fields! Behold why ruin is in the house! Naught do you with shiftless fingers but steal the bread of your own relation!"

Azénor's anger was like milk that boils upon the fire, as soon as it boils it overflows the pot. From reproaches Azénor went to threats and then from threats to blows. Téphany, at the irate woman's onslaught, burst into sobs and you can guess what was her amazement, when she beheld each tear become a round and shining pearl.

Old Mother Bourhis, uttering a cry of admiration, began to snatch them up.

Dénès too, arriving, stared with eyes like saucers.

"Pearls! pearls!" he cried out in excitement.

"It's a fortune for us," babbled Azénor who continued to sweep them up in handfuls. "No one else must know about this, Dénès. Weep on, Téphany, weep on!"

She held out her apron and Dénès his hat. He was thinking only about the pearls, and had forgotten they were his sweetheart's tears. Thus can mere sight of wealth befuddle wits of men!

"Alack, alack the tears are stopping!" Azénor now explained. "By all the saints, Téphany if I had luck like yours I would out-weep the very rains from Heaven! Shall we beat her, Dénès, and bring her sobs again?"

"No, no," broke in Dénès, "we mustn't wear her out the first time. As for me I shall start for town at once and find out what each pearl is worth."

"And I shall go with you!" cried Azénor, and the two hastily left the house.

Téphany, alone at last, clasped her hands upon her heart. In anguish she raised her eyes to Heaven, then dropped them to the dark chimney corner where suddenly she saw again the wrinkled beggar woman. The crone's regard was bent upon her with a strange and mocking smile. The girl started, then with a gesture of despair, held out toward the fairy the pin, the feather and the box of ointment.

"Take them back!" Téphany cried. "Woe to people who are not content with gifts that God has granted. Give other girls wit, beauty, wealth; I wish to be again the simple-hearted girl I was."

The smile broadened on the old crone's face, "That is right, Téphany," said she, "you have learned much through your ordeal. I was sent to give you this lesson, and now you will live happily for ever after."

At these words, the beggar woman was changed into a sparkling fairy. Light flooded the cottage and she disappeared in a cloud, sweetly scented with violets and rose.

Téphany forgave Dénès for having wished to sell her tears, and as they were both no longer hard to please, they were as happy as it is possible to be upon this earth. She married the lad from Plover, and he was always the devoted husband that her heart had longed to have.

THE ADVENTURE of CHERRY of ZENNOR

Cornwall

Old Honey lived with his wife and family in a little hut of two rooms and a "talfat,"[1] on the cliff side of Trereen in Zennor. The old couple had half-a-score of children, who were all reared in this place. They lived as they best could on the produce of a few acres of ground, which were too poor to keep even a goat in good heart. The heaps of crogans[2] about the hut led one to believe that their chief food was limpets and gweans.[3] They had, however, fish and potatoes most days, and pork and broth now and then of a Sunday. At Christmas and the Feast they had white bread. There was not a healthier nor a handsomer family in the parish than Old Honey's. We are, however, only concerned with one of them—his daughter Cherry. Cherry could run as fast as a hare, and was ever full of frolic and mischief.

Whenever the miller's boy came into the "town," tied his horse to the furze-rick and called in to see if any one desired to send corn to the mill, Cherry would jump on to its back and gallop off to the cliff. When the miller's boy gave chase, and she could ride no further over the edge of that rocky coast, she would take to the cairns, and the swiftest dog could not catch her, much less the miller's boy.

Soon after Cherry got into her teens she became very discontented, because year after year her mother had been promising her a new frock that she might go

---

1. *Talfat* is a half-floor at one end of a cottage on which a bed is placed.
2. limpet-shells
3. periwinkles

off as smart as the rest, "three on one horse to Morva Fair."[4] As certain as the time came round the money was wanting, so Cherry had nothing decent. She could neither go to fair, nor to church, nor to meeting.

Cherry was sixteen. One of her playmates had a new dress smartly trimmed with ribbons, and she told Cherry how she had been to Nancledry to the preaching, and how she had ever so many sweethearts who brought her home. This put the volatile Cherry in a fever of desire. She declared to her mother she would go off to the "low countries"[5] to seek for service, that she might get some clothes like other girls.

Her mother wished her to go to Towednack, that she might have the chance of seeing her now and then of a Sunday.

"No, no!" said Cherry, "I'll never go to live in the parish where the cow ate the bell-rope, and where they have fish and taties[6] every day, and conger-pie of a Sunday for a change."

One fine morning Cherry tied up a few things in a bundle and prepared to start. She promised her father that she would get service as near home as she could, and come home at the earliest opportunity. The old man said she was bewitched, charged her to take care she wasn't carried away by either the sailors or pirates, and allowed her to depart. Cherry took the road leading to Ludgvan and Gulval. When she lost sight of the chimneys of Trereen, she got out of heart, and had a great mind to go home again. But she went on.

At length she came to the four cross roads on the Lady Downs, sat herself down on a stone by the roadside, and cried to think of her home, which she might never see again.

Her crying at last came to an end, and she resolved to go home and make the best of it.

When she dried her eyes and held up her head she was surprised to see a gentleman coming towards her;—for she couldn't think where he came from; no one was to be seen on the Downs a few minutes before.

---

4. a Cornish proverb
5. The terms "high" and "low countries" are applied respectively to the hills and the valleys of the country about Towednack and Zennor.
6. potatoes

The gentleman wished her "Good morning," inquired the road to Towednack, and asked Cherry where she was going.

Cherry told the gentleman that she had left home that morning to look for service, but that her heart had failed her, and she was going back over the hills to Zennor again.

"I never expected to meet with such luck as this," said the gentleman. "I left home this morning to seek for a nice clean girl to keep house for me, and here you are."

He then told Cherry that he had been recently left a widower, and that he had one dear little boy, of whom Cherry might have charge. Cherry was the very girl that would suit him. She was handsome and cleanly. He could see that her clothes were so mended that the first piece could not be discovered; yet she was as sweet as a rose, and all the water in the sea could not make her cleaner. Poor Cherry said "Yes, sir," to everything, yet she did not understand one quarter part of what the gentleman said. Her mother had instructed her to say "Yes, sir," to the parson, or any gentleman, when, like herself, she did not understand them. The gentleman told her he lived but a short way off, down in the low countries; that she would have very little to do but milk the cow and look after the baby; so Cherry consented to go with him.

Away they went, he talking so kindly that Cherry had no notion how time was moving, and she quite forgot the distance she had walked.

At length they were in lanes, so shaded with trees that a checker of sunshine scarcely gleamed on the road. As far as she could see, all was trees and flowers. Sweetbriars and honeysuckles perfumed the air, and the reddest of ripe apples hung from the trees over the lane.

Then they came to a stream of water as clear as crystal, which ran across the lane. It was, however, very dark, and Cherry paused to see how she should cross the river. The gentleman put his arm around her waist and carried her over, so that she did not wet her feet.

The lane was getting darker and darker, and narrower and narrower, and they seemed to be going rapidly down-hill.

Cherry took firm hold of the gentleman's arm, and thought, as he had been so kind to her, she could go with him to the world's end.

After walking a little farther, the gentleman opened a gate which led into a beautiful garden, and said, "Cherry, my dear, this is the place we live in."

Cherry could scarcely believe her eyes. She had never seen anything approaching this place for beauty. Flowers of every dye were around her; fruits of all kinds hung above her; and the birds, sweeter of song than any she had ever heard, burst out into a chorus of rejoicing. She had heard granny tell of enchanted places. Could this be one of them? No. The gentleman was as big as the parson; and now a little boy came running down the garden-walk shouting, "Papa, papa."

The child appeared, from his size, to be about two or three years of age; but there was a singular look of age about him. His eyes were brilliant and piercing, and he had a crafty expression. As Cherry said, "He could look anybody down."

Before Cherry could speak to the child, a very old, dry-boned, ugly-looking woman made her appearance, and seizing the child by the arm, dragged him into the house, mumbling and scolding. Before, however, she was lost sight of, the old hag cast one look at Cherry, which shot through her heart "like a gimblet."

Seeing Cherry somewhat disconcerted, the master explained that the old woman was his late wife's grandmother; that she would remain with them until Cherry knew her work, and no longer, for she was old and ill-tempered, and must go. At length, having feasted her eyes on the garden, Cherry was taken into the house, and this was yet more beautiful. Flowers of every kind grew everywhere, and the sun seemed to shine everywhere, and yet she did not see the sun.

Aunt Prudence—so was the old woman named—spread a table in a moment with a great variety of nice things, and Cherry made a hearty supper. She was now directed to go to bed, in a chamber at the top of the house, in which the child was to sleep also. Prudence directed Cherry to keep her eyes closed, whether she could sleep or not, as she might, perchance, see things which she would not like. She was not to speak to the child all night. She was to rise at break of day; then take the boy to a spring in the garden, wash him, and anoint his eyes with an ointment, which she would find in a crystal box in a cleft of the rock, but she was not, on any account, to touch her own eyes with it. Then Cherry was to call the cow; and having taken a bucket full of milk, to draw a bowl of the last milk for the boy's breakfast. Cherry was dying with curiosity. She several times began to question the child, but he always stopped her with, "I'll tell Aunt Prudence." According to her orders, Cherry was up in the morning early. The little boy conducted the girl to the spring, which flowed in crystal purity from a granite rock, which was covered with ivy and beautiful mosses. The child was duly washed, and his eyes duly anointed. Cherry saw no cow, but her little charge said she must call the cow.

"Pruit! pruit! pruit!" called Cherry, just as she would call the cows at home; when, lo! a beautiful great cow came from amongst the trees, and stood on the bank beside Cherry.

Cherry had no sooner placed her hands on the cow's teats than four streams of milk flowed down and soon filled the bucket. The boy's bowl was then filled, and he drank it. This being done, the cow quietly walked away, and Cherry returned to the house to be instructed in her daily work.

The old woman, Prudence, gave Cherry a capital breakfast, and then informed her that she must keep to the kitchen, and attend to her work there—to scald the milk, make the butter, and clean all the platters and bowls with water and gard.[7] Cherry was charged to avoid curiosity. She was not to go into any other part of the house; she was not to try and open any locked doors.

After her ordinary work was done on the second day, her master required Cherry to help him in the garden, to pick the apples and pears, and to weed the leeks and onions.

Glad was Cherry to get out of the old woman's sight. Aunt Prudence always sat with one eye on her knitting, and the other boring through poor Cherry. Now and then she'd grumble, "I knew Robin would bring down some fool from Zennor—better for both that she had tarried away."

Cherry and her master got on famously, and whenever Cherry had finished weeding a bed, her master would give her a kiss to show her how pleased he was.

After a few days, old Aunt Prudence took Cherry into those parts of the house which she had never seen. They passed through a long dark passage. Cherry was then made to take off her shoes; and they entered a room, the floor of which was

---

7. gravel sand

like glass, and all round, perched on the shelves, and on the floor, were people, big and small, turned to stone. Of some, there were only the head and shoulders, the arms being cut off; others were perfect. Cherry told the old woman she "wouldn't come any further for all the world." She thought from the first she was got into a land of Small People underground, only master was like other men; but now she knew she was with the conjurors, who had turned all these people to stone. She had heard talk on them up in Zennor, and she knew they might at any moment wake up and eat her.

Old Prudence laughed at Cherry, and drove her on, insisted upon her rubbing up a box, "like a coffin on six legs," until she could see her face in it. Well, Cherry did not want for courage, so she began to rub with a will; the old woman standing by, knitting all the time, calling out every now and then, "Rub! rub! rub! harder and faster!" At length Cherry got desperate, and giving a violent rub at one of the corners, she nearly upset the box. When, O Lord! it gave out such a doleful, unearthly sound, that Cherry thought all the stone-people were coming to life, and with her fright she fell down in a fit. The master heard all this noise, and came in to inquire into the cause of the hubbub. He was in great wrath, kicked old Prudence out of the house for taking Cherry into that shut-up room, carried Cherry into the kitchen, and soon, with some cordial, recovered her senses. Cherry could not remember what had happened; but she knew there was something fearful in the other part of the house. But Cherry was mistress now—old Aunt Prudence was gone. Her master was so kind and loving that a year passed by like a summer day. Occasionally her master left home for a season; then he would return and spend much time in the enchanted apartments, and Cherry was certain she had heard him talking to the stone-people. Cherry had everything the human heart could desire, but she was not happy; she would know more of the place and the people. Cherry had discovered that the ointment made the little boy's eyes bright and strange, and she thought often that he saw more than she did; she would try, yes, she would!

Well, next morning the child was washed, his eyes anointed, and the cow milked; she sent the boy to gather her some flowers in the garden, and taking a "crum" of ointment, she put it into her eye. Oh, her eye would be burned out of her head! Cherry ran to the pool beneath the rock to wash her burning eye; when lo! she saw at the bottom of the water, hundreds of little people, mostly ladies, playing,—and there was her master, as small as the others, playing with them. Everything now looked different about the place. Small people were everywhere, hiding in the flowers sparkling with diamonds, swinging in the trees, and running and leaping under and over the blades of grass. The master never showed himself above the water all day; but at night he rode up to the house like the handsome gentleman she had seen before. He went to the enchanted chamber and Cherry soon heard the most beautiful music.

In the morning, her master was off, dressed as if to follow the hounds. He returned at night, left Cherry to herself, and proceeded at once to his private apartments. Thus it was day after day, until Cherry could stand it no longer. So she peeped through the keyhole, and saw her master with lots of ladies, singing; while one dressed like a queen was playing on the coffin. Oh, how madly jealous Cherry became when she saw her master kiss this lovely lady! However, the next day, the master remained at home to gather fruit. Cherry was to help him, and when, as usual, he looked to kiss her, she slapped his face, and told him to kiss the Small People, like himself, with whom he played under the water. So he found out that Cherry had used the ointment. With much sorrow he told her she must go home,—that he would have no spy on his actions, and that Aunt Prudence must come back. Long before day, Cherry was called by her master. He gave her lots of clothes and other things;—took her bundle in one hand, and a lantern in the other, and bade her follow him. They went on for miles on miles, all the time going up hill, through lanes, and narrow passages. When they came at last on level ground, it was near daybreak. He kissed Cherry, told her she was punished for her idle curiosity; but that he would, if she behaved well, come sometimes on the Lady Downs to see her. Saying this, he disappeared. The sun rose, and there was Cherry seated on a granite stone, without a soul within miles of her,—a desolate moor having taken the place of a smiling garden. Long, long did Cherry sit in sorrow, but at last she thought she would go home.

Her parents had supposed her dead, and when they saw her, they believed her to be her own ghost. Cherry told her story, which every one doubted, but Cherry never varied her tale, and at last every one believed it. They say Cherry was never afterwards right in her head, and on moonlight nights, until she died, she would wander on to the Lady Downs to look for her master.

NEAR AND FAR

TE KANAWA'S ADVENTURE with a TROOP of FAIRIES

Aotearoa (New Zealand)

Te Kanawa, a chief of Waikato, was the man who fell in with a troop of fairies upon the top of Puke-more, a high hill in the Waikato district.

This chief happened one day to go out to catch kiwis with his dogs, and when night came on he found himself right at the top of Puke-more. So his party made a fire to give them light, for it was very dark. They had chosen a tree to sleep under—a very large tree, the only one fit for their purpose that they could find; in fact, it was a very convenient sleeping-place, for the tree had immense roots, sticking up high above the ground; they slept between these roots, and made the fire beyond them.

As soon as it was dark they heard loud voices, like the voices of people coming that way; there were the voices of men, of women, and of children, as if a very large party of people were coming along. They looked for a long time, but could see nothing; till at last Te Kanawa knew the noise must proceed from fairies. His people were all dreadfully frightened, and would have run away if they could; but where could they run to, for they were in the midst of a forest, on the top of a lonely mountain, and it was dark night.

For a long time the voices grew louder and more distinct as the fairies drew nearer and nearer, until they came quite close to the fire; Te Kanawa and his party were half dead with fright. At last the fairies approached to look at Te Kanawa, who was a very handsome fellow. To do this, they kept peeping slily over the large roots of the tree under which the hunters were lying, and kept constantly looking at Te Kanawa, whilst his companions were quite insensible from fear. Whenever the fire blazed up brightly, off went the fairies and hid themselves, peeping out from behind stumps and trees; and when it burnt low, back they came close to it, merrily singing as they moved—

> "Here you come climbing over Mount Tirangi
> To visit the handsome chief of Ngapuhi,
> Whom we have done with."[1]

A sudden thought struck Te Kanawa, that he might induce them to go away if he gave them all the jewels he had about him; so he took off a beautiful little figure, carved in green jasper, which he wore as a neck ornament, and a precious carved jasper ear-drop from his ear. Ah, Te Kanawa was only trying to amuse and please them to save his life, but all the time he was nearly frightened to death. However, the fairies did not rush on the men to attack them, but only came quite close to look at them. As soon as Te Kanawa had taken off his neck ornament, and pulled out his jasper ear-ring, and his other ear-ring, made of a tooth of the tiger-shark, he spread them out before the fairies, and offered them to the multitude who were sitting all round about the place; and thinking it better the fairies should not touch him, he took a stick, and fixing it into the ground, hung his neck ornament and ear-rings upon it.

As soon as the fairies had ended their song, they took the shadows of the ear-rings, and handed them about from one to the other, until they had passed through the whole party, which then suddenly disappeared, and nothing more was seen of them.

The fairies carried off with them the shadows of all the jewels of Te Kanawa, but they left behind them his jasper neck ornament and his ear-rings, so that he took them back again, the hearts of the fairies being quite contented at getting the shadows alone; they saw, also, that Te Kanawa was an honest, well-dispositioned fellow. However, the next morning, as soon as it was light, he got down the mountain as fast as he could without stopping to hunt longer for kiwis.

---

1. Te Wherowhero, the storyteller, did not remember the whole song, but that this was the concluding verse; it was probably in allusion to their coming to peep at Te Kanawa.

THE IMP of the WELL

Turkey

Once there lived a woodcutter who, besides his poverty, had nothing but a most cantankerous wife. All the money this poor man earned, his wife took from him, so that he had never a single para for himself. When the supper was too salty—and this happened very often—if the man dared to say, "You have oversalted the food, mother!" he might be quite certain that the next day there would not be so much as a pinch of salt in it. Now if he dared to say, "You have forgotten the salt, mother!" on the following day it would be so salty that he would be unable to eat it. It once happened to this poor man that he kept back a piastre from his wages, intending to buy a rope. His wife found this out, and began to scold him furiously. "But, my dear," said the woodcutter gently, "I only wanted the money to buy a rope. Do not be so violent." "What I have done to you hitherto is as nothing to what I intend to do," snapped the woman, and sprang at him, whereon a great uproar ensued, and how either escaped with their life is more than I can understand.

Next morning the husband, determined to endure it no longer, saddled an ass and went into the mountains. All he said to his wife was that she must not follow him. He had not been gone long, however, before she also got upon an ass and set off after him. "Who knows," she mumbled to herself, "what he will be up to if I am not with him?" Presently the man became aware that his wife was behind him, but he pretended not to notice her. When he arrived in the mountains he immediately set to work woodcutting. The woman walked to and fro restlessly, examining every nook and corner; only an old well escaped her vigilant eye, and she was upon it before anyone could have stopped her. "Take care!" shouted her husband; "mind the well! Come back!" But the woman paid no heed to the warning, though she heard well enough. Another step, she lost her balance, then presto! she found herself at the bottom of the well. Her husband, deciding she was not worth troubling about further, bestrode his ass and went home.

Next day he returned to his work in the mountains, and, thinking of his wife, he said to himself: "I will just see what has happened to the poor woman." Going to the top of the well he peeped down, but could see no trace of her. He now repented his unfeeling conduct of the previous day, reflecting that, though a shrew, she was after all his wife. What could have become of her? He took a rope, let it down the well, and shouted: "Take hold of the rope, mother, and I will pull you up." Presently the man perceived by the tightening of the rope that some one had grasped it, and he commenced to haul with all his might. He pulled away until he was nearly exhausted, and brought to the surface—a horrible imp! The miserable woodcutter was terribly frightened. "Fear me not, poor man," said the imp. "May the Almighty bless you for your deed. You have rescued me from great peril, and I shall always remember your kindness." Astounded, the poor man inquired the nature of the peril from which he had chanced to rescue the imp.

"For many years," answered the imp, "I had lived peacefully in this old well. Until last night nothing had ever happened to disturb the calm of my existence. Then an old woman fell down upon me. She seized me by the ears, and held on so tightly that I could not free myself from her grasp. By good fortune, when you let down the rope, I was the first to seize it—praised be the most merciful Allah! For your kindness I will reward you."

So saying, the imp brought forth three leaves, and gave them to the woodcutter. "I will now creep into the Sultan's daughter," he proceeded. "She will then become very ill. They will send for physicians and hodjas, but all will be in vain. When you hear of it, go to the Padishah, and produce these three leaves. As soon as you touch her face with them I will come out of her; she will be restored to health, and you will be richly rewarded."

The woodcutter, who considered this a capital plan, now parted from the imp, and gave no further thought to his wife in the well.

No sooner had the imp left the woodcutter than he went direct to the palace of the Padishah, and crept into the Sultan's daughter. The poor Princess broke out into loud and constant cries of "My head! Oh, my head!" The monarch, being told of this sudden malady, visited his afflicted daughter, and was grieved to find her in such dreadful pain. Physicians and hodjas without number were sent for, but all their skill was of no avail; the maiden continued to shriek, "Oh, my head!" "My darling," said her father, "hearing your cries of suffering causes me pain almost as great as your own. What can be done? I will call the astrologers—perhaps they can tell us." All the most famous astrologers of the land came, consulted the stars, and prescribed each a different medicine; but the Princess grew worse and worse.

To return to the woodcutter. He managed quite well without his wife, and soon forgot her. He had nearly forgotten the imp and the leaves as well, when one day he heard the Padishah's proclamation. "My daughter is sick unto death," it ran. "Physicians, hodjas, and astrologers have failed to heal her. Whoever can render help, let him come and render it. If he be a Muslim he shall receive my daughter in marriage now, and my kingdom at my death; or, if he be an unbeliever, all the treasures of my kingdom shall be his."

This reminded the woodcutter of the imp and the three leaves. He went to the palace and undertook by the aid of Allah to cure the Princess. The Padishah led him without delay into the chamber of his sick daughter, who was still crying, "Oh, my head! my head!" The woodcutter produced the three leaves, moistened them, and pressed them on the patient's forehead, when the pain instantly departed and she was as well as though she had never known illness. Then there was great rejoicing in the serai. The Sultan's daughter became the bride of the poor woodcutter, who was henceforth the Padishah's son-in-law.

Our Padishah had a good friend in the Padishah of the adjoining kingdom, whose daughter also was in the power of the Imp of the Well. She suffered from the same complaint, and the physicians and hodjas were just as helpless in her case as in the other. Now our Padishah informed his friend of his own good fortune and offered to send his son-in-law, who, by the grace of Allah, would no doubt be able to restore the daughter of his friend.

Accordingly the Padishah made known to his son-in-law what he desired. Though the latter had great misgiving, he could not well refuse; so he set forth on his journey to the court of the neighbouring country. Immediately on arrival he was taken to the sick Princess, and soon realised that he had again to do with the Imp of the Well.

"Once you did me a favour," said the imp, "but now you cannot say I am your debtor. I delivered the Sultan's daughter into your hands and sought another for myself; would you take this one also from me? If you do, I will take your Princess from you."

The poor man was terribly perplexed, but resolved to try the effect of a trick. "I have not come for the maid," said he, "she is your lawful property; if you wish you may have mine also." "Then what do you here?" demanded the imp. "The woman—the woman in the well," groaned the former woodcutter, "she was my wife; I left her in the well to be rid of her." The imp showed signs of uneasiness, and asked: "Has she got out of the well?" "Yes, more's the pity!" sighed the man. "She follows me about wherever I go. Now she is there—behind the door!" That was enough to frighten the imp; he lost no time in quitting the Sultan's daughter. He left the town in all haste, without waiting to learn if the woodcutter spoke the truth, and was never heard of again. Thus the Princess recovered and henceforth lived very happily.

RIQUET with the TUFT

France

Once upon a time there was a Queen who had a son, so ugly and misshapen, that it was doubted for a long time whether his form was really human. A fairy, who was present at his birth, affirmed, nevertheless, that he would be worthy to be loved, as he would have an excellent wit; she added, moreover, that by virtue of the gift she had bestowed upon him, he would be able to impart equal intelligence to the one whom he loved best. All this was some consolation to the poor Queen, who was much distressed at having brought so ugly a little monkey into the world. It is true that the child was no sooner able to speak than he said a thousand pretty things, and that in all his ways there was a certain air of intelligence, with which everyone was charmed. I had forgotten to say that he was born with a little tuft of hair on his head, and so he came to be called Riquet with the Tuft; for Riquet was the family name.

About seven or eight years later, the Queen of a neighbouring kingdom had two daughters. The elder was fairer than the day, and the Queen was so delighted, that it was feared some harm might come to her from her great joy. The same fairy who had assisted at the birth of little Riquet, was present upon this occasion, and in order to moderate the joy of the Queen, she told her that this little Princess would have no gifts of mind at all, and that she would be as stupid as she was beautiful. The Queen was greatly mortified on hearing this, but, shortly after, she was even more annoyed, when her second little daughter was born and proved to be extremely ugly. "Do not distress yourself, madam," said the fairy to her, "your daughter will find compensation, for she will have so much intelligence, that her lack of beauty will scarcely be perceived."

"Heaven send it may be so," replied the Queen; "but are there no means whereby a little more understanding might be given to the elder, who is so lovely?" "I can do nothing for her in the way of intelligence, madam," said the fairy, "but everything in the way of beauty; as, however, there is nothing in my power I would not do to give you comfort, I will bestow on her the power of conferring beauty on any man or woman who shall please her." As these two Princesses grew up, their endowments also became more perfect, and nothing was talked of anywhere but the beauty of the elder, and the intelligence of the younger. It is true that their defects also greatly increased with their years. The younger became uglier every moment, and the elder more stupid every day. She either made no answer when she was spoken to, or else said something foolish. With this she was so clumsy, that she could not even place four pieces of china on a mantelshelf, without breaking one of them, or drink a glass of water, without spilling half of it on her dress. Notwithstanding the attraction of beauty, the younger, in whatever society they might be, nearly always bore away the palm from her sister. At first everyone went up to the more beautiful, to gaze at and admire her; but they soon left her for the cleverer one, to listen to her many pleasant and amusing sayings; and people were astonished to find that in less than a quarter of an hour, the elder had not a soul near her, while all the company had gathered round the younger. The elder, though very stupid, noticed this, and would have given, without regret, all her beauty, for half the sense of her sister. Discreet as she was, the Queen could not help often reproaching her with her stupidity, which made the poor Princess ready to die of grief.

One day, when she had gone by herself into a wood, to weep over her misfortune, she saw approaching her, a little man of very ugly and unpleasant appearance, but magnificently dressed. It was the young Prince Riquet with the Tuft, who, having fallen in love with her from seeing her portraits, which were sent all over the world, had left his father's kingdom that he might have the pleasure of beholding her and speaking to her. Enchanted at meeting her thus alone, he addressed her with all the respect and politeness imaginable. Having remarked, after paying her the usual compliments, that she was very melancholy, he said to her, "I cannot understand, madam, how a person so beautiful as you are can be so unhappy as you appear; for, although I can boast of having seen an infinite number of beautiful people, I can say with truth that I have never seen one whose beauty could be compared with yours."

"You are pleased to say so, sir," replied the Princess, and there she stopped.

"Beauty," continued Riquet, "is so great an advantage, that it ought to take the place of every other, and, possessed of it, I see nothing that can have power to afflict one."

"I would rather," said the Princess, "be as ugly as you are, and have intelligence, than possess the beauty I do, and be so stupid as I am."

"There is no greater proof of intelligence, madam, than the belief that we have it not; it is the nature of that gift, that the more we have, the more we believe ourselves to be without it."

"I do not know how that may be," said the Princess, "but I know well enough that I am very stupid, and that is the cause of the grief that is killing me."

"If that is all that troubles you, madam, I can easily put an end to your sorrow."

"And how would you do that?" said the Princess.

"I have the power, madam," said Riquet with the Tuft, "to give as much intelligence as it is possible to possess, to the person whom I love best; as you, madam, are that person, it will depend entirely upon yourself, whether or not you become gifted with this amount of intelligence, provided that you are willing to marry me."

The Princess was struck dumb with astonishment, and replied not a word.

"I see," said Riquet with the Tuft, "that this proposal troubles you, and I am not surprised, but I will give you a full year to consider it."

The Princess had so little sense, and at the same time was so anxious to have a great deal, that she thought the end of that year would never come; so she at once accepted the offer that was made her. She had no sooner promised Riquet with the Tuft that she would marry him that day twelve months, than she felt herself quite another person to what she had previously been. She found she was able to say whatever she pleased, with a readiness past belief, and of saying it in a clever, but easy and natural manner. She immediately began a sprightly and well-sustained conversation with Riquet with the Tuft, and was so brilliant in her talk, that Riquet with the Tuft began to think he had given her more wit than he had reserved for himself. On her return to the palace, the whole Court was puzzled to account for a change so sudden and extraordinary; for the number of foolish things which they had been accustomed to hear from her, she now made as many sensible and exceedingly witty remarks. All the Court was in a state of joy not to be described. The younger sister alone was not altogether pleased, for, having lost her superiority over her sister in the way of intelligence, she now only appeared by her side as a very unpleasing-looking person.

The King now began to be guided by his elder daughter's advice, and at times even held his Council in her apartments. The news of the change of affairs was spread abroad, and all the young princes of the neighbouring kingdoms exerted themselves to gain her affection, and nearly all of them asked her hand in marriage. She found none of them, however, intelligent enough to please her, and she listened to all of them, without engaging herself to one.

At length arrived a Prince, so rich and powerful, so clever and so handsome, that she could not help listening willingly to his addresses. Her father, having perceived this, told her that he left her at perfect liberty to choose a husband for herself, and that she had only to make known her decision. As the more intelligence we possess, the more difficulty we find in making up our mind on such a matter as this, she begged her father, after having thanked him, to allow her time to think about it.

She went, by chance, to walk in the same wood in which she had met Riquet with the Tuft, in order to meditate more uninterruptedly over what she had to do. While she was walking, deep in thought, she heard a dull sound beneath her feet, as of many persons running to and fro, and busily occupied. Having listened more attentively, she heard one say, "Bring me that saucepan;" another, "Give me that kettle;" another, "Put some wood on the fire." At the same moment the ground opened, and she saw beneath her what appeared to be a large kitchen, full of cooks, scullions, and all sorts of servants necessary for the preparation of a magnificent banquet. There came forth a band of about twenty to thirty cooks, who went and established themselves in an avenue of the wood, at a very long table, and who, each with the larding-pin in his hand and the tail of his fur cap over his ear, set to work, keeping time to a harmonious song.

The Princess, astonished at this sight, asked the men for whom they were working.

"Madam," replied the chief among them, "for Prince Riquet with the Tuft, whose marriage will take place to-morrow." The Princess, still more surprised than she was before, and suddenly recollecting that it was just a twelvemonth from the day on which she had promised to marry Prince Riquet with the Tuft, was overcome with trouble and amazement. The reason of her not having remembered her promise was, that when she made it she had been a very foolish person, and when she became gifted with the new mind that the Prince had given her, she had forgotten all her follies.

She had not taken another thirty steps, when Riquet with the Tuft presented himself before her, gaily and splendidly attired, like a Prince about to be married. "You see, madam," said he, "I keep my word punctually, and I doubt not that you have come thither to keep yours, and to make me, by the giving of your hand, the happiest of men."

"I confess to you, frankly," answered the Princess, "that I have not yet made up my mind on that matter, and that I do not think I shall ever be able to do so in the way you wish." "You astonish me, madam," said Riquet with the Tuft. "I have no doubt I do," said the Princess; "and assuredly, had I to deal with a stupid person, with a man without intelligence, I should feel greatly perplexed. 'A Princess is bound by her word,' he would say to me, 'and you must marry me, as you have promised to do so.' But as the person to whom I speak is, of all men in the world, the one of greatest sense and understanding, I am certain he will listen to reason. You know that, when I was no better than a fool, I nevertheless could not decide to marry you—how can you expect, now that I have the mind which you have given me, and which renders me much more difficult to please than before, that I should take to-day a resolution which I could not then? If you seriously thought of marrying me, you did very wrong to take away my stupidity, and so enable me to see more clearly than I saw then."

"If a man without intelligence," replied Riquet with the Tuft, "who reproached you with your breach of promise, might have a right, as you have just intimated, to be treated with indulgence, why would you, madam, that I should receive less consideration in a matter which affects the entire happiness of my life? Is it reasonable that persons of intellect should be in a worse position than those that have none? Can you assert this—you who have so much, and who so earnestly desired to possess it? But let us come to the point, if you please. Setting aside my ugliness, is there anything in me that displeases you? Are you dissatisfied with my birth, my understanding, my temper, or my manners?"

"Not in the least," replied the Princess; "I admire in you everything you have mentioned."

"If that is so," rejoined Riquet with the Tuft, "I shall soon be happy, as you have it in your power to make me the most pleasing looking of men."

"How can that be done?" asked the Princess.

"It can be done," said Riquet with the Tuft, "if you love me sufficiently to wish that it should be. And, in order, madam, that you should have no doubt about it, know that the same fairy, who, on the day I was born, endowed me with the power to give intelligence to the person I chose, gave you also the power to render handsome the man you should love, and on whom you should wish to bestow this favour."

"If such be the fact," said the Princess, "I wish, with all my heart, that you should become the handsomest and most lovable Prince in the world, and I bestow the gift on you to the fullest extent in my power."

The Princess had no sooner pronounced these words than Riquet with the Tuft appeared to her eyes, of all men in the world, the handsomest, the best made, and most attractive she had ever seen. There are some who assert that it was not the spell of the fairy, but love alone that caused this metamorphosis. They say that the Princess, having reflected on the perseverance of her lover, on his prudence, and on all the good qualities of his heart and mind, no longer saw the deformity of his body, or the ugliness of his features; that his hump appeared to her nothing more than a good-natured shrug of his shoulders, and that instead of noticing, as she had done, how badly he limped, she saw in him only a certain lounging air, which charmed her. They say also that his eyes, which squinted, only seemed to her the more brilliant for this; and that the crookedness of his glance was to her merely expressive of his great love; and, finally, that his great red nose had in it, to her mind, something martial and heroic. However this may be, the Princess promised on the spot to marry him, provided he obtained the consent of the King, her father. The King, having learned that his daughter entertained a great regard for Riquet with the Tuft, whom he knew also to be a very clever and wise Prince, received him with pleasure as his son-in-law. The wedding took place the next morning, as Riquet with the Tuft had foreseen, and according to the orders which he had given a long time before.

No beauty, no talent, has power above
Some indefinite charm discern'd only by love.

THE STORY of AOYAGI

Japan

In the era of Bunmei (1469–1486) there was a young samurai called Tomotada in the service of Hatakéyama Yoshimuné, the Lord of Noto.[1] Tomotada was a native of Echizen;[2] but at an early age he had been taken, as page, into the palace of the daimyō of Noto, and had been educated, under the supervision of that prince, for the profession of arms. As he grew up, he proved himself both a good scholar and a good soldier, and continued to enjoy the favor of his prince. Being gifted with an amiable character, a winning address, and a very handsome person, he was admired and much liked by his samurai-comrades.

When Tomotada was about twenty years old, he was sent upon a private mission to Hosokawa Masamoto, the great daimyō of Kyōto, a kinsman of Hatakéyama Yoshimuné. Having been ordered to journey through Echizen, the youth requested and obtained permission to pay a visit, on the way, to his widowed mother.

It was the coldest period of the year when he started; the country was covered with snow; and, though mounted upon a powerful horse, he found himself obliged to proceed slowly. The road which he followed passed through a mountain-district where the settlements were few and far between; and on the second day of his journey, after a weary ride of hours, he was dismayed to find that he could not reach his intended halting-place until late in the night. He had reason to be

---

1. An ancient province corresponding to the northern part of present-day Ishikawa Prefecture.
2. An ancient province corresponding to the eastern part of present-day Fukui Prefecture.

anxious;—for a heavy snowstorm came on, with an intensely cold wind; and the horse showed signs of exhaustion. But, in that trying moment, Tomotada unexpectedly perceived the thatched roof of a cottage on the summit of a near hill, where willow-trees were growing. With difficulty he urged his tired animal to the dwelling; and he loudly knocked upon the storm-doors, which had been closed against the wind. An old woman opened them, and cried out compassionately at the sight of the handsome stranger: "Ah, how pitiful!—a young gentleman traveling alone in such weather! Deign, young master, to enter."

Tomotada dismounted, and after leading his horse to a shed in the rear, entered the cottage, where he saw an old man and a girl warming themselves by a fire of bamboo splints. They respectfully invited him to approach the fire; and the old folks then proceeded to warm some rice-wine, and to prepare food for the traveler, whom they ventured to question in regard to his journey. Meanwhile the young girl disappeared behind a screen. Tomotada had observed, with astonishment, that she was extremely beautiful,—though her attire was of the most wretched kind, and her long, loose hair in disorder. He wondered that so handsome a girl should be living in such a miserable and lonesome place.

The old man said to him:—

"Honored Sir, the next village is far; and the snow is falling thickly. The wind is piercing; and the road is very bad. Therefore, to proceed further this night would probably be dangerous. Although this hovel is unworthy of your presence, and although we have not any comfort to offer, perhaps it were safer to remain to-night under this miserable roof. We would take good care of your horse."

Tomotada accepted this humble proposal,—secretly glad of the chance thus afforded him to see more of the young girl. Presently a coarse but ample meal was set before him; and the girl came from behind the screen, to serve the wine. She was now reclad, in a rough but cleanly robe of homespun; and her long, loose hair had been neatly combed and smoothed. As she bent forward to fill his cup, Tomotada was amazed to perceive that she was incomparably more beautiful than any woman whom he had ever before seen; and there was a grace about her every motion that astonished him. But the elders began to apologize for her, saying:

"Sir, our daughter, Aoyagi,[3] has been brought up here in the mountains, almost alone; and she knows nothing of gentle service. We pray that you will pardon her stupidity and her ignorance." Tomotada protested that he deemed himself lucky to be waited upon by so comely a maiden. He could not turn his eyes away from her—though he saw that his admiring gaze made her blush;—and he left the wine and food untasted before him. The mother said: "Kind Sir, we very much hope that you will try to eat and to drink a little,—though our peasant-fare is of the worst,—as you must have been chilled by that piercing wind." Then, to please the old folks, Tomotada ate and drank as he could; but the charm of the blushing girl still grew upon him. He talked with her, and found that her speech was sweet as her face. Brought up in the mountains she might have been;—but, in that case, her parents must at some time have been persons of high degree; for she spoke and moved like a damsel of rank. Suddenly he addressed her with a poem—which was also a question—inspired by the delight in his heart:—

> "Tadzunétsuru,
> Hana ka toté koso,
> Hi wo kurasé,
> Akénu ni otoru
> Akané sasuran?"

> [*"Being on my way to pay a visit, I found that which I took to be a flower: therefore here I spend the day. . . . Why, in the time before dawn, the dawn-blush tint should glow—that, indeed, I know not."*][4]

Without a moment's hesitation, she answered him in these verses:—

---

3. The name signifies "Green Willow;"—though rarely met with, it is still in use.
4. The poem may be read in two ways; several of the phrases having a double meaning. But the art of its construction would need considerable space to explain. The meaning which Tomotada desired to convey might be thus expressed:—"While journeying to visit my mother, I met with a being lovely as a flower; and for the sake of that lovely person, I am passing the day here. . . . Fair one, wherefore that dawn-like blush before the hour of dawn?—can it mean that you love me?"

"Izuru hi no
Honoméku iro wo
Waga sodé ni
Tsutsumaba asu mo
Kimiya tomaran."

[*"If with my sleeve I hide the faint fair color of the dawning sun,—then, perhaps, in the morning my lord will remain."*][5]

Then Tomotada knew that she accepted his admiration; and he was scarcely less surprised by the art with which she had uttered her feelings in verse, than delighted by the assurance which the verses conveyed. He was now certain that in all this world he could not hope to meet, much less to win, a girl more beautiful and witty than this rustic maid before him; and a voice in his heart seemed to cry out urgently, "Take the luck that the gods have put in your way!" In short he was bewitched—bewitched to such a degree that, without further preliminary, he asked the old people to give him their daughter in marriage,—telling them, at the same time, his name and lineage, and his rank in the train of the Lord of Noto.

They bowed down before him, with many exclamations of grateful astonishment. But, after some moments of apparent hesitation, the father replied:—

"Honored master, you are a person of high position, and likely to rise to still higher things. Too great is the favor that you deign to offer us;—indeed, the depth of our gratitude therefore is not to be spoken or measured. But this girl of ours, being a stupid country-girl of vulgar birth, with no training or teaching of any sort, it would be improper to let her become the wife of a noble samurai. Even to speak of such a matter is not right. But, since you find the girl to your liking, and have condescended to pardon her peasant-manners and to overlook her great rudeness, we do gladly present her to you, for a humble handmaid. Deign, therefore, to act hereafter in her regard according to your august pleasure."

Ere morning the storm had passed; and day broke through a cloudless east. Even if the sleeve of Aoyagi hid from her lover's eyes the rose-blush of that dawn,

---

5. Another reading is possible; but this one gives the signification of the *answer* intended.

he could no longer tarry. But neither could he resign himself to part with the girl; and, when everything had been prepared for his journey, he thus addressed her parents:—

"Though it may seem thankless to ask for more than I have already received, I must once again beg you to give me your daughter for wife. It would be difficult for me to separate from her now; and as she is willing to accompany me, if you permit, I can take her with me as she is. If you will give her to me, I shall ever cherish you as parents. And, in the meantime, please to accept this poor acknowledgment of your kindest hospitality."

So saying, he placed before his humble host a purse of gold ryō. But the old man, after many prostrations, gently pushed back the gift, and said:—

"Kind master, the gold would be of no use to us; and you will probably have need of it during your long, cold journey. Here we buy nothing; and we could not spend so much money upon ourselves, even if we wished. As for the girl, we have already bestowed her as a free gift;—she belongs to you: therefore it is not necessary to ask our leave to take her away. Already she has told us that she hopes to accompany you, and to remain your servant so long as you may be willing to endure her presence. We are only too happy to know that you deign to accept her; and we pray that you will not trouble yourself on our account. In this place we could not provide her with proper clothing,—much less with a dowry. Moreover, being old, we should in any event have to separate from her before long. Therefore it is very fortunate that you should be willing to take her with you now."

It was in vain that Tomotada tried to persuade the old people to accept a present: he found that they cared nothing for money. But he saw that they were really anxious to trust their daughter's fate to his hands; and he therefore decided to take her with him. So he placed her upon his horse, and bade the old folks farewell for the time being, with many sincere expressions of gratitude.

"Honored Sir," the father made answer, "it is we, and not you, who have reason for gratitude. We are sure that you will be kind to our girl; and we have no fears for her sake."

Now a samurai was not allowed to marry without the consent of his lord; and Tomotada could not expect to obtain this sanction before his mission had been accomplished. He had reason, under such circumstances, to fear that the beauty of Aoyagi might attract dangerous attention, and that means might be devised of taking her away from him. In Kyōto he therefore tried to keep her hidden from curious eyes. But a retainer of Lord Hosokawa one day caught sight of Aoyagi, discovered her relation to Tomotada, and reported the matter to the daimyō. Thereupon the daimyō—a young prince, and fond of pretty faces—gave orders that the girl should be brought to the place; and she was taken thither at once, without ceremony.

Tomotada sorrowed unspeakably; but he knew himself powerless. He was only a humble messenger in the service of a far-off daimyō; and for the time being he was at the mercy of a much more powerful daimyō, whose wishes were not to be questioned. Moreover Tomotada knew that he had acted foolishly,—that he had brought about his own misfortune, by entering into a clandestine relation which the code of the military class condemned. There was now but one hope for him,—a desperate hope: that Aoyagi might be able and willing to escape and to flee with him. After long reflection, he resolved to try to send her a letter. The attempt would be dangerous, of course: any writing sent to her might find its way to the hands of the daimyō; and to send a love-letter to any inmate of the place was an unpardonable offense. But he resolved to dare the risk; and, in the form of a Chinese poem, he composed a letter which he endeavored to have conveyed to her. The poem was written with only twenty-eight characters. But with those twenty-eight characters he was able to express all the depth of his passion, and to suggest all the pain of his loss:—[6]

Kōshi ō-son gojin wo ou;
Ryokuju namida wo tarété rakin wo hitataru;
Komon hitotabi irité fukaki koto umi no gotoshi;
Koré yori shorō koré rojin.

---

6. So the Japanese story-teller would have us believe,—although the verses seem commonplace in translation. I have tried to give only their general meaning: an effective literal translation would require some scholarship.

[*Closely, closely the youthful prince now follows after the gem-bright maid;—*
The tears of the fair one, falling, have moistened all her robes.
But the august lord, having once become enamored of her—the depth of his longing is like the depth of the sea.
Therefore it is only I that am left forlorn,—only I that am left to wander alone.]

On the evening of the day after this poem had been sent, Tomotada was summoned to appear before the Lord Hosokawa. The youth at once suspected that his confidence had been betrayed; and he could not hope, if his letter had been seen by the daimyō, to escape the severest penalty. "Now he will order my death," thought Tomotada;—"but I do not care to live unless Aoyagi be restored to me. Besides, if the death-sentence be passed, I can at least try to kill Hosokawa." He slipped his swords into his girdle, and hastened to the palace.

On entering the presence-room he saw the Lord Hosokawa seated upon the dais, surrounded by samurai of high rank, in caps and robes of ceremony. All were silent as statues; and while Tomotada advanced to make obeisance, the hush seemed to him sinister and heavy, like the stillness before a storm. But Hosokawa suddenly descended from the dais, and, taking the youth by the arm, began to repeat the words of the poem:—"*Kōshi ō-son gojin wo ou.*" And Tomotada, looking up, saw kindly tears in the prince's eyes.

Then said Hosokawa:—

"Because you love each other so much, I have taken it upon myself to authorize your marriage, in lieu of my kinsman, the Lord of Noto; and your wedding shall now be celebrated before me. The guests are assembled;—the gifts are ready."

At a signal from the lord, the sliding-screens concealing a further apartment were pushed open; and Tomotada saw there many dignitaries of the court, assembled for the ceremony, and Aoyagi awaiting him in bride's apparel. Thus was she given back to him;—and the wedding was joyous and splendid;—and precious gifts were made to the young couple by the prince, and by the members of his household.

For five happy years, after that wedding, Tomotada and Aoyagi dwelt together. But one morning Aoyagi, while talking with her husband about some household matter, suddenly uttered a great cry of pain, and then became very white and still. After a few moments she said, in a feeble voice: "Pardon me for thus rudely crying out—but the pain was so sudden! . . . My dear husband, our union must have been brought about through some Karma-relation in a former state of existence; and that happy relation, I think, will bring us again together in more than one life to come. But for this present existence of ours, the relation is now ended;—we are about to be separated. Repeat for me, I beseech you, the *Nembutsu*-prayer,—because I am dying."

"Oh! what strange wild fancies!" cried the startled husband,—"you are only a little unwell, my dear one! Lie down for a while, and rest; and the sickness will pass."

"No, no!" she responded—"I am dying!—I do not imagine it;—I know! . . . And it were needless now, my dear husband, to hide the truth from you any longer:—I am not a human being. The soul of a tree is my soul;—the heart of a tree is my heart;—the sap of the willow is my life. And some one, at this cruel moment, is cutting down my tree;—that is why I must die! . . . Even to weep were now beyond my strength!—quickly, quickly repeat the *Nembutsu* for me . . . quickly! . . . Ah!"

With another cry of pain she turned aside her beautiful head, and tried to hide her face behind her sleeve. But almost in the same moment her whole form appeared to collapse in the strangest way, and to sink down, down, down—level with the floor. Tomotada had sprung to support her;—but there was nothing to support! There lay on the matting only the empty robes of the fair creature and the ornaments that she had worn in her hair: the body had ceased to exist.

Tomotada shaved his head, took the Buddhist vows, and became an itinerant priest. He traveled through all the provinces of the empire; and, at all the holy places which he visited, he offered up prayers for the soul of Aoyagi. Reaching Echizen, in the course of his pilgrimage, he sought the home of the parents of his beloved. But when he arrived at the lonely place among the hills, where their dwelling had been, he found that the cottage had disappeared. There was nothing to mark even the spot where it had stood, except the stumps of three willows—two old trees and one young tree—that had been cut down long before his arrival.

Beside the stumps of those willow-trees he erected a memorial tomb, inscribed with divers holy texts; and he there performed many Buddhist services on behalf of the spirits of Aoyagi and of her parents.

THE HERD-BOY

Sweden

There was once a poor herd-boy, who had neither kith nor kin except his stepmother, who was a wicked woman, and hardly allowed him food or clothing. Thus the poor boy suffered great privation; during all the livelong day he had to tend cattle, and scarcely ever got more than a morsel of bread morning and evening.

One day his stepmother had gone out without leaving him any food; he had, therefore, to drive his cattle to the field fasting, and being very hungry, he wept bitterly. But at the approach of noon he dried his tears, and went up on a green hill, where he was in the habit of resting, while the sun was hot in the summer. On this hill it was always cool and dewy under the shady trees; but now he remarked that there was no dew, that the ground was dry, and the grass trampled down. This seemed to him very singular, and he wondered who could have trodden down the green grass. While thus sitting and thinking, he perceived something that lay glittering in the sunshine. Springing up to see what it might be, he found it was a pair of very, very small shoes of the whitest and clearest glass. The boy now felt quite happy again, forgot his hunger, and amused himself the whole day with the little glass shoes.

In the evening, when the sun had sunk behind the forest, the herd-boy called his cattle and drove them to the village. When he had gone some way, he was met by a very little boy, who in a friendly tone greeted him with “Good evening!” “Good evening again,” answered the herd-boy. “Hast thou found my shoes, which I lost this morning in the green grass?" asked the little boy. The herd-boy answered: "Yes, I have found them; but, my good little fellow, let me keep them. I intended to give them to my stepmother, and then, perhaps, I should have got a little meat, when I came home." But the boy prayed so earnestly, "Give me back my shoes; another time I will be as kind to thee," that the herd-boy returned him the shoes. The little one then, greatly delighted, gave him a friendly nod, and went springing away.

The herd-boy now collected his cattle together, and continued his way homewards. When he reached his dwelling it was already dark, and his stepmother chided him for returning so late. "There's still some porridge in the pot," said she; "eat now, and pack thyself off to bed, so that thou canst get up in the morning betimes, like other folks." The poor herd-boy durst not return any answer to these hard words, but ate, and then slunk to bed in the hayloft, where he was accustomed to sleep. The whole night he dreamed of nothing but the little boy and his little glass shoes.

Early in the morning, before the sun shone from the east, the boy was waked by his stepmother's voice: "Up with thee, thou sluggard! It is broad day, and the animals are not to stand hungry for thy sloth." He instantly rose, got a bit of bread, and drove the cattle to the pasture.

When he came to the green hill, which was wont to be so cool and shady, he again wondered to see that the dew was all swept from the grass, and the ground dry, even more so than on the preceding day. While he thus sat thinking, he observed something lying in the grass and glittering in the bright sunshine. Springing towards it, he found it was a very, very little red cap set round with small golden bells. At this he was greatly delighted, forgot his hunger, and amused himself all day with the little elegant cap.

In the evening, when the sun had sunk behind the forest, the herd-boy gathered his cattle together, and drove them towards the village. When on his way, he was met by a very little and, at the same time, very fair damsel. She greeted him in a friendly tone with "Good evening!" "Good evening again," answered the lad. The damsel then said: "Hast thou found my cap, which I lost this morning in the green grass?" The boy answered: "Yes, I have found it; but let me keep it, my pretty maid. I thought of giving it to my wicked stepmother, and then, perhaps, I shall get a little meat when I go home." But the little damsel entreated so urgently, "Give me back my cap; another time I will be as good to thee," that the lad gave her the little cap, when she appeared highly delighted, gave him a friendly nod, and sprang off.

On his return home, he was received as usual by his cruel stepmother, and dreamed the whole night of the little damsel and her little red cap.

In the morning he was turned out fasting, and on coming to the hill, found it was drier than on either of the preceding days, and that the grass was trodden down in large rings. It then entered his mind all that he had heard of the little elves, how in the summer nights they were wont to dance in the dewy grass, and he found that these must be elfin-rings, or elfin-dances. While sitting absorbed in thought, he chanced to strike his foot against a little bell that lay in the grass, and which gave forth so sweet a sound, that all the cattle came running together, and stood still to listen. Now the boy was delighted, and could do nothing but play with the little bell, till he forgot his troubles and the cattle forgot to graze. And so the day passed much more quickly than can be imagined.

When it drew towards evening, and the sun was level with the tree-tops, the boy called his cattle and prepared to return home. But let him entice and call them as he might, they were not to be drawn from the pasture, for it was a delightful grassy spot. Then thought the boy to himself, "Perhaps they will pay more heed to the little bell." So drawing forth the bell, he tingled it as he went along the way. In one moment the bell-cow came running after him, and was followed by the rest of the herd. At this the boy was overjoyed, for he was well aware what an advantage the little bell would be to him. As he was going on, a very little old man met him, and kindly bade him a good evening. "Good evening again," said the boy. The old man asked: "Hast thou found my little bell, which I lost this morning in the green grass?" The herd-boy answered: "Yes, I have found it." The old man said: "Then give it me back."

"No," answered the boy, "I am not so doltish as you may think. The day before yesterday I found two small glass shoes, which a little boy wheedled from me. Yesterday I found a cap, which I gave to a little damsel; and now you come to take from me the little bell, which is so good for calling the cattle. Other finders get a reward for their pains, but I get nothing." The little man then used many fair words, with the view of recovering his bell, but all to no purpose. At last he said: "Give me back the little bell, and I will give thee another, with which thou mayest call thy cattle; thou shalt, moreover, obtain three wishes." These seemed to the boy no unfavourable terms, and he at once ageed to them, adding, "As I may wish whatever I will, I will wish to be a king, and I will wish to have a great palace, and also a very beautiful queen."

"Thou hast wished no trifling wishes," said the old man, "but bear well in mind what I now tell thee. To-night, when all are sleeping, thou shalt go hence, till thou comest to a royal palace, which lies due north. Take this pipe of bone. If thou fallest into trouble, blow it; if thou afterwards fallest into great trouble, blow it again; but if, on a third occasion, thou findest thyself in still greater peril, break the pipe in two, and I will help thee, as I have promised." The boy gave the old man many thanks for his gifts, and the elf-king—for it was he—went his way. But the boy bent his steps homewards, rejoicing as he went along, that he should so soon escape from tending cattle for his wicked stepmother.

When he reached the village it was already dark, and his stepmother had been long awaiting his coming. She was in a great rage, so that the poor lad got blows instead of food. "This will not last long," thought the boy, comforting himself with the reflection, as he went up to his hayloft, where he laid himself down and slumbered for a short time. About midnight, long before the cock crew, he arose, slipped out of the house, and began his journey in a northward direction, as the old man had enjoined. He travelled incessantly, over hill and dale, and twice did the sun rise and twice set, while he was still on his way.

Towards evening on the third day he came to a royal palace, which was so spacious that he thought he should never again see the like. He went to the kitchen and asked for employment. "What dost thou know, and what canst thou do?" inquired the master-cook. "I can tend cattle in the pasture," answered the boy. The master-cook said: "The king is in great want of a herd-boy; but it will, no doubt, be with thee as with the others, that every day thou losest one of the herd." The boy answered: "Hitherto I have never lost any beast that I drove to the field." He was then taken into the king's service, and tended the king's cattle; but the wolf never got a beast from him: so he was well esteemed by all the king's servants.

One evening, as the herd-boy was driving his cattle home, he observed a beautiful young damsel standing at a window and listening to his song. Though he seemed hardly to notice her, he, nevertheless, felt a glow suffused over him. Some time passed in this manner, the herd-boy being delighted every time he saw the young maiden; though he was still ignorant that she was the king's daughter. It happened one day that the young girl came to him as he was driving the herd to their pasture. She had with her a little snow-white lamb, and begged him in a friendly tone to take charge of her lamb, and protect it from the wolves in the forest. At this the herd-boy was so confused that he could neither answer nor speak. But he took the lamb with him, and found his greatest pleasure in guarding it, and the animal attached itself to him, as a dog to its master. From that day the herd-boy frequently enjoyed the sight of the fair princess. In the morning, when he drove his cattle to the pasture, she would stand at the window listening to his song; but in the evening, when he returned from the forest, she would descend to caress her little lamb, and say a few friendly words to the herd-boy.

Time rolled on. The herd-boy had grown up into a comely, vigorous young man; and the princess had sprung up and was become the fairest maiden that could be found far or near. Nevertheless, she came every evening, according to her early custom, to caress her lamb. But one day the princess was missing and could nowhere be found. This event caused a great sorrow and commotion in the royal court, for the princess was beloved by every one: but the king and queen, as was natural, grieved the most intensely of all. The king sent forth a proclamation over the whole land, that whosoever should recover his daughter should be rewarded with her hand and half the kingdom. This brought a number of princes, and knights, and warriors from the east and the west. Cased in steel they rode forth with arms and attendants, to seek the lost princess; but few were they that returned from their wanderings, and those that did return brought no tidings of her they went in quest of. The king and queen were now inconsolable, and thought that they had sustained an irreparable loss. The herd-boy, as before, drove his cattle to the pasture, but it was in sadness, for the king's fair daughter engrossed his thoughts every day and every hour.

One night in a dream the little elfin king seemed to stand before him and to say: "To the north! to the north! there thou wilt find thy queen." At this the young man was so overjoyed that he sprang up, and as he woke, there stood the little man, who nodded to him, and repeated: "To the north! to the north!" He then vanished, leaving the youth in doubt whether or not it were an illusion. As soon as it was day he went to the hall of the palace, and requested an audience of the king. At this all the royal servants wondered, and the master-cook said: "Thou hast served for so many years that thou mayest, no doubt, get thy wages increased without speaking to the king himself." But the young man persisted in his request, and let it be understood that he had something very different in his mind. On entering the royal apartment, the king demanded his errand, when the young man said: "I have served you faithfully for many years, and now desire permission to go and seek for the princess." Hereupon the king grew angry and said: "How canst thou, a herd-boy, think of doing that which no warrior nor prince has been able to accomplish?" But the youth answered boldly, that he would either discover the princess or, for her sake, lay down his life. The king then let his anger pass, and called to mind the old proverb: *A heart worthy of scarlet often lies under a coarse woollen cloak.* He therefore gave orders that the herd-boy should be equipped with a charger and all things requisite. But the youth said: "I reck not of riding; give me but your word and permission, together with means sufficient." The king then wished him success in his enterprise; but all the boys and other servants in the court laughed at the herd-boy's rash undertaking.

The young man journeyed towards the north, as he had been instructed by the elf-king, and proceeded on and on until he could not be far distant from the world's end. When he had thus travelled over mountains and desolate ways, he came at length to a great lake, in the midst of which there was a fair island, and on the island a royal palace, much more spacious than the one from whence he came. He went down to the water's edge, and surveyed the palace on every side. While thus viewing it, he perceived a damsel with golden locks standing at one of the windows, and making signs with a silken band, such as the princess's lamb was accustomed to wear. At this sight the young man's heart leaped in his breast; for it rushed into his mind that the damsel could be no other than the princess herself.

He now began to consider how he should cross over the water to the great palace; but could hit upon no plan. At last the thought occurred to him that he would make a trial whether the little elves would afford him some assistance; and he took forth his pipe, and blew a long-continued strain. He had scarcely ceased, when he heard a voice behind him, saying "Good evening." "Good evening again," answered the youth, turning about; when just before him there stood the little boy whose glass shoes he had found in the grass. "What dost thou wish of me?" asked the elfin boy. The other answered: "I wish thee to convey me across the water to the royal palace." The boy replied: "Place thyself on my back." The youth did so; and at the same instant the boy changed his form and became an immensely huge hawk, that darted through the air, and stopped not until it reached the island, as the young man had requested.

He now went up to the hall of the palace and asked for employment. "What dost thou understand and what canst thou do?" inquired the master-cook. "I can take charge of cattle," answered the youth. The master-cook then said: "The giant is just now in great want of a herdsman; but it will, I dare say, be with thee as with the others; for if a beast by chance is lost, thy life is forfeited." The youth answered: "This seems to me a hard condition; but I will, nevertheless, agree to it." The master-cook then accepted his service, and he was to commence on the following day.

The young man now drove the giant's cattle, and sung his song, and rang his little bell, as he had formerly done; and the princess sat at her window, and listened, and made signs to him that he should not appear to notice her. In the evening he drove the herd from the forest, and was met by the giant, who said to him: "Thy life is in the place of any one that may be missing." But not a beast was wanting, let the giant count them as he would. Now the *Tusse*[1] was quite friendly, and said: "Thou shalt be my herdsman all thy days." He then went down to the lake, loosed his enchanted ship, and rowed thrice round the island, as he was wont to do.

---

1. The same as Thurs, one of the old denominations of a giant.

During the giant's absence the princess stationed herself at the window and sang:—

"To-night, to-night, thou herdsman bold,
Goes the cloud from under my star.
And if thou comest hither, then will I be thine,
My crown I will gladly give thee."

The young man listened to her song, and understood from it that he was to go in the night and deliver the princess. He therefore went away without appearing to notice anything. But when it was late, and all were sunk in deep sleep, he stealthily approached the tower, placed himself before the window, and sang:—

"To-night will wait thy herdsman true,
Will sad stand under thy window;
And if thou comest down, thou mayest one day be mine,
While the shadows fall so widely."

The princess whispered: "I am bound with chains of gold, come and break them." The young man now knew no other course than again to blow with his pipe a very long-continued strain; when instantly he heard a voice behind him, saying "Good evening." "Good evening again," answered the youth, looking round; when there stood the little elf-king, from whom he had got the little bell and the pipe. "What wilt thou with me?" inquired the old man. The young man answered: "I beseech you to convey me and the princess hence." The little man said: "Follow me." They then ascended to the maiden's tower: the castle gate opened spontaneously, and when the old man touched the chain, it burst in fragments. All three then went down to the margin of the lake, when the elf-king sang:—

"Thou little pike in the water must go,
Come, come, hastily!
A princess fair on thy back shall ride,
And eke a king so mighty."

At the same moment appeared the little damsel, whose cap the herd-boy had found in the grass. She sprang down to the lake, and was instantly changed into a large pike that sported about in the water. Then said the elf-king: "Sit ye on the back of the pike. But the princess must not be terrified, let what may happen; for then will my power be at an end." Having so said, the old man vanished; but the youth and the fair princess followed his injunctions, and the pike bore them rapidly along through the billows.

While all this was taking place, the giant awoke, looked through the window, and perceived the herd-boy floating on the water together with the young princess. Instantly snatching up his eagle-plumage,[2] he flew after them. When the pike heard the clapping of the giant's wings, it dived far down under the surface of the water, whereat the princess was so terrified that she uttered a scream. Then was the elf-king's power at an end, and the giant seized the two fugitives in his talons. On his return to the island he caused the young herdsman to be cast into a dark dungeon, full fifteen fathoms underground; but the princess was again placed in her tower, and strictly watched, lest she should again attempt to escape.

The youth now lay in the captives' tower, and was in deep affliction at finding himself unable to deliver the princess, and, at the same time, having most probably forfeited his own life. The words of the elfin king now occurred to his memory: "If, on a third occasion, thou findest thyself in great peril, break the pipe in two, and I will help thee." As a last resource, therefore, he drew forth the little pipe and broke it in two. At the same moment he heard behind him the words "Good evening." "Good evening again," answered the youth; and when he looked round there stood the little old man close by him, who asked: "What wilt thou with me?" The young man answered: "I wish to deliver the princess, and to convey her home to her father." The old man then led him through many locked doors and many splendid apartments, till they came to a spacious hall, filled with all kinds of weapons, swords, spears, and axes, of which some shone like polished steel, others like burnished gold. The old man kindled a fire on the hearth, and said: "Undress thyself!" The young man did so, and the little man burnt his old garments. He then went to a large iron chest, out of which he took a costly suit of

---

2. A complete Eddaic giant.

armour, resplendent with the purest gold. "Dress thyself," said he: the young man did so. When he was thus armed from head to foot, the old man bound a sharp sword by his side, and said: "It is decreed that the giant shall fall by this sword, and this armour no steel can penetrate." The young herdsman felt quite at ease in the golden armour, and moved as gracefully as if he had been a prince of the highest degree. They then returned to the dark dungeon; the youth thanked the elf-king for his timely succour, and they parted from each other.

Till a late hour there was a great bustle and hurrying in the whole palace; for the giant was on that day to celebrate his marriage with the beautiful princess, and had invited many of his kin to the feast. The princess was clad in the most sumptuous manner, and decorated with a crown and rings of gold, and other costly ornaments, which had been worn by the giant's mother. The health of the wedded pair was then drunk amid all kinds of rejoicing, and there was no lack of good cheer, both of meat and drink. But the bride wept without intermission, and her tears were so hot that they felt like fire on her cheeks.

When night approached, and the giant was about to conduct his bride to the nuptial chamber, he sent his pages to fetch the young herdsman, who lay in the dungeon. But when they entered the prison, the captive had disappeared, and in his stead there stood a bold warrior, with sword in hand, and completely armed. At this apparition the young men were frightened and fled; but were followed by the herdsman, who thus ascended to the court of the palace, where the guests were assembled to witness his death. When the giant cast his eyes on the doughty warrior, he was exasperated, and exclaimed: "Out upon thee, thou base Troll!" As he spoke his eyes became so piercing that they saw through the young herdsman's armour; but the youth fearless said: "Here shalt thou strive with me for thy fair bride." The giant was not inclined to stay, and was about to withdraw; but the herdsman drew his sword, which blazed like a flame of fire. When the giant recognised the sword, under which he was doomed to fall, he was terror-struck and sank on the earth; but the young herdsman advanced boldly, swung round his sword, and struck a blow so powerful that the giant's head was separated from his carcase. Such was his end.

On witnessing this exploit, the wedding-guests were overcome with fear, and departed, each to his home; but the princess ran forth and thanked the brave herdsman for having saved her. They then proceeded to the water, loosed the giant's enchanted ship, and rowed away from the island. On their arrival at the king's court, there was great joy that the king had recovered his daughter, for whom he had mourned so long. There was afterwards a sumptuous wedding, and the young herdsman obtained the king's fair daughter. They lived happily for very many years, and had many beautiful children. The bell and the broken pipe are preserved as memorials, aye even to the present day.

A NOTE ON THE SOURCES

The stories in this book were collected, translated, and published in the late nineteenth and early twentieth centuries. They have been excerpted from the publications listed on the following pages, all of which are in the public domain.

In almost all cases, the stories are presented in their original format. For "Whippety-Stourie," "The White Trout," and "The Adventure of Cherry of Zennor," we have removed phonetic spelling that was used to suggest dialect. And for "An Orkney Selkie Story," we have adjusted both phonetic spelling and some specific archaic or local terms that might not be comprehensible to modern readers.

Most of these tales originate from Ireland, Scotland, England, Wales, or Brittany—all places associated with fairies and fae folk. However, in the final section we have expanded our lens to include stories from other parts of the world. The magical figures in these tales are not exactly equivalent to the fairies of Celtic or Anglo-Saxon cultures, and the use of the term "fairy" to describe them may originate with the folklorists who wrote down these stories rather than the original storytellers.

However, they share many characteristics with fairies: a deep connection to nature, a beguiling aspect or personality, and a strict adherence to their own arcane rules. Depending on the protagonist's actions, these figures can either offer great blessings or make life a misery.

Our hope is that reading this book not only deepens your appreciation of Celtic and Anglo-Saxon lore, but also encourages you to explore other, equally wonderful folktale traditions. The additional volumes in our Tales series are a great place to start.

SOURCES

"The Elfin Knight"
Grierson, Elizabeth W. *The Scottish Fairy Book*. Reprint of the J. B. Lippincott Company 1910 Philadelphia edition, Internet Archive, 2007. https://archive.org/details/scottishfairyboo00grie/page/n8

"Owain of Drws Coed"
Henderson, Bernard and Stephen Jones. *Wonder Tales of Ancient Wales*. Reprint of the Small, Maynard & Company 1921 Boston edition, Internet Archive, 2007. https://archive.org/details/wondertalesofanc00hendiala/page/n11/mode/2up

"Tamlane"
Jacobs, Joseph. *More English Fairy Tales*. Reprint of the G. P. Putnam's Sons 1894 New York edition, Internet Archive, 2007. https://archive.org/details/moreenglishfairy00jaco/page/n7/mode/2up

"Childe Rowland"
Steel, Flora Annie. *English Fairy Tales*. Reprint of the Macmillan & Co. 1922 New York edition, Internet Archive, 2008. https://archive.org/details/englishfairytales00stee/page/n9/mode/2up

"The Fairies of Merlin's Crag"
Grierson, Elizabeth W., *The Scottish Fairy Book*. Reprint of the J. B. Lippincott Company 1910 Philadelphia edition, Internet Archive, 2007. https://archive.org/details/scottishfairyboo00grie/page/n8

"Fairy Cows" (told by William Keating)
Curtin, Jeremiah. *Tales of the Fairies and of the Ghost World.* Reprint of the Little, Brown & Company 1895 Boston edition, Internet Archive, 2009. https://archive.org/details/talesfairiesand00curtgoog/page/n9

"The Brewery of Egg-Shells" (told by T. Crofton Croker)
Yeats, William Butler. *Fairy and Folk Tales of the Irish Peasantry.* Reprint of the Walter Scott Publishing Co. c. 1890 London edition, Internet Archive, 2007. https://archive.org/details/fairyfolktalesof00yeat/page/n1/mode/2up

"The Fairies of Rahonain and Elizabeth Shea" (told by John Malone)
Curtin, Jeremiah. *Tales of the Fairies and of the Ghost World.* Reprint of the Little, Brown & Company 1895 Boston edition, Internet Archive, 2009. https://archive.org/details/talesfairiesand00curtgoog/page/n9

"Whippety-Stourie"
Grierson, Elizabeth W., *The Scottish Fairy Book.* Reprint of the J. B. Lippincott Company 1910 Philadelphia edition, Internet Archive, 2007. https://archive.org/details/scottishfairyboo00grie/page/n8

"An Orkney Selkie Story"
Dennison, Walter Traill. "Orkney Folk-Lore" from *The Scottish Antiquary, or, Northern Notes and Queries*, volume VII. Reprint of the T. and A. Constable 1893 Edinburgh edition, pages 173–177, Google Books. https://books.google.com/books?id=8EYGSax2tSgC&pg=PA171#v=onepage&q&f=true

"The White Trout" (told by S. Lover)
Yeats, William Butler. *Fairy and Folk Tales of the Irish Peasantry.* Reprint of the Walter Scott Publishing Co. c. 1890 London edition, Internet Archive, 2007. https://archive.org/details/fairyfolktalesof00yeat/page/n1/mode/2up

"The Four Gifts"
Masson, Elsie. *Folk Tales of Brittany*. Reprint of the Macrae Smith Company 1929 Philadelphia edition, Sacred Texts, 2004. https://sacred-texts.com/neu/celt/ftb/index.htm

"The Adventure of Cherry of Zennor"
Hunt, Robert. *Popular Romances of the West of England, or the Drolls, Traditions, and Superstitions of Old Cornwall*, third edition. Reprint of the Chatto & Windus 1908 London edition, Internet Archive, 2007. https://archive.org/details/popularromanceso00huntuoft/page/n11/mode/2up

"Te Kanawa's Adventure with a Troop of Fairies" (told by Te Wherowhero)
Grey, Sir George. *Polynesian Mythology and Ancient Traditional History of the New Zealand Race, as Furnished by Their Priests and Chiefs*. Reprint of the John Murray 1855 London edition. Internet Archive, 2017. https://archive.org/details/in.ernet.dli.2015.219427/page/n3/mode/2up.

"The Imp of the Well"
Kúnos, Ignácz. *Fourty-Four Turkish Fairy Tales*. Reprint of the George C. Harrap & Co 1913 London edition, Internet Archive, 2007. https://archive.org/details/fortyfourturkish001862/page/n5/mode/2up

"Riquet with the Tuft"
Perrault, Charles. *Tales of Passed Times*. Reprint of the J. M. Dent & Company 1900 London edition, Internet Archive, 2008. https://archive.org/details/talesofpassedtim00perrrich/page/n9/mode/2up

"The Story of Aoyagi"
Hearn, Lafcadio. *Kwaidan: Stories and Studies of Strange Things*. Reprint of the Houghton Mifflin Company 1911 Boston and New York edition, Internet Archive, 2013. https://archive.org/details/kwaidanstoriesst00hear

"The Herd-Boy"

Yule-Tide Stories: A Collection of Scandinavian and North German Popular Tales and Traditions from the Swedish, Danish, and German. Edited by Benjamin Thorpe. Reprint of the George Bell & Sons 1910 London edition, Internet Archive, 2007. https://archive.org/details/yuletidestoriesc00thor